NOT MY SHADOW

A SHADOW SEALS NOVEL

ELAINE LEVINE

Published by Elaine Levine
Copyright © 2022 Elaine Levine
Last Updated: February 16, 2022
Cover art by Cat Johnson
Editing by Arran McNicol @ editing720
Proofreading by Jenn @ bookendsediting.com

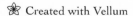 Created with Vellum

NOT MY SHADOW
SHADOW SEALS

A Mission Gone Awry

A wounded friend's inexplicable death gets Navy SEAL Nash Thompson entangled in a mystery with hooks all the way up his chain of command. His enemies not only shut all doors on him, they board them up and nail them closed, leaving him out of a job, a home, a future. Even his brotherhood shuns him, proving he's gotten too close to the criminal ring of thugs he's been hunting. Run to ground, there's just one path open to him — a quid pro quo deal offered by a shadow vigilante that provides him a lead in his investigation in exchange for his help in a decade-old case the FBI hasn't been able to close — one eerily similar to his own investigation.

It's shady as hell, but it offers him the justice he's after.

Who Doesn't Have Secrets?

An ex they hope to never see again...an error in judgment that haunts them...a past they can't put behind them. Annie Bergen has eaten a cold diet of shame her entire life. Harmony Falls is where she went to hide and maybe start living again, if she can put her life back together. But the guy with the scarred hand who comes to the diner makes her realize this is where she'll die...

Until another man shows up, one with hard eyes, secrets as dark as her own, and a shadow big enough to hide hers.

Shadow SEALs

Cat Johnson Shadow Pawn
Elle James Shadow Assassin
Becca Jameson Shadow in the Desert
KaLyn Cooper Shadow in the Mountain
Donna Michaels Shadow of a Chance
JM Madden Shadow of the Moon
Sharon Hamilton Shadow of the Heart
Abbie Zanders Cast in Shadow
Elaine Levine Not My Shadow
Cat Johnson Shadow Lies
Donna Michaels Shadow of Hope
Elaine Levine Shadow and Steele
JM Madden Shadow Games
Sharon Hamilton Shadow Warrior
KaLyn Cooper Shadow in the Daylight
Becca Jameson Shadow in the Darkness

OTHER BOOKS BY ELAINE LEVINE

Sleeper SEALs

Romantic Suspense/Military Suspense

(This series may be read in any order.)

Men of Defiance Series

Historical Western Romance

(This series may be read in any order.)

DEDICATION

1

Annie drove down the short stretch of Harmony Falls' Old Town, feeling the cold sweat of a rising panic. She'd tried, for half her life, to move beyond what had happened nearby, but the more she pushed the memories and pain down, the more it sucked her down with it.

Starting over was a conscious decision, a necessary one if she wanted to have any semblance of a life. But coming back here, where it all began, might be yet another bad choice in a decade of them.

Harmony Falls itself was starting over. It had been a polygamous community, closed to the outside world, until just a few years ago. Annie didn't have a thing against consenting adults choosing to live an open life-style, but that wasn't what had been happening here. The system was structured to idolize its male leaders and subjugate its female population. The group's leadership had been found guilty of various felonies, including child abuse, sex trafficking, and RICO offenses. Its latest "prophet," a U.S. senator, known to the group as Josiah, had died mysteriously a couple of years ago.

After the sect was broken up, the town's population dropped to a quarter of what it had been when Annie was first there, fourteen years ago. Right, wrong, or indifferent, the townspeople had saved her once. Now Harmony Falls was the exact kind of place she'd been looking for. Small. Forgotten. Quiet. A place like that could give a ravaged heart some peace...but that wasn't why she was here.

She made two passes down the main road, looking for a "Help Wanted" sign. No one seemed to be hiring, and her odds of finding work were slim—many of the storefronts were empty. She didn't have time to delay getting situated. Staying in hotels while she tried to figure out her new beginning was depleting her modest savings. It was possible she could do what she needed to while commuting from another nearby town. If Harmony Falls wasn't where she could live and work, she was going to have to decide that today.

She parked in front of the little grocery store—the only one of its kind for miles around. A couple of other cars were parked out front, but there were blocks of empty, angled parking spots around them. She went inside. A middle-aged man stood behind one of two register stations. He checked her over critically, then nodded at her and returned his attention to the customer in his line.

Annie walked around the store, selecting some

things she could cook in her hotel room's microwave. She went down the coffee aisle and filled her lungs with the scent of freshly ground coffee. What she wouldn't give to wake up to the smell of freshly brewed coffee waiting for her—one of many things she'd given up in this wild plan of hers.

When her arms were full, she brought her items to the checkout.

The man looked at her basic selection of goods and said, "I haven't seen you around."

"I'm new here. I'm thinking of staying."

"Why?"

"Why not? Seems like a lovely place. I thought it might be affordable."

"It's gonna be a ghost town soon. If I were you, I'd just move along."

Annie sighed. "I can't. I'm about out of money."

The man grunted and began bagging her items.

"Any chance you know of anyone hiring around here?" Annie asked. "Are you?"

He scoffed. "You're one of a dozen or so customers I'm gonna have today. Yeah, I'd love some help, but I don't really need it. I already have a part-time employee."

"Oh."

"But the diner across the street might have something open. Betty's my sister—and my main customer. While things are slow here, she's got enough locals coming in to keep the lights on, which helps me keep mine on. Why not go have a chat with her? Tell her I sent you."

Annie paid him, then lifted her bag and held it close. "Thank you. I will." She started for the exit, then paused. "I didn't get your name."

"Bernie Carson."

"I'm Annie. Nice to meet you."

She dropped her groceries off in her Jeep, pausing a moment to regroup before making her next appeal for a job. If Bernie's sister said no, then she'd have to move on to the next town. And the next and the next, until eventually, someone somewhere would have a job for her. Maybe she should find a campground and stay there. It would be cheaper to sleep in her car than in a motel, and a campground might have shower facilities.

She crossed the street and went into the diner. The hours posted outside read, *Open 6 am to 2 pm, Monday through Saturday*. She went inside.

Trying to act casual and not appear desperate, she ordered the cheapest thing on the menu: grilled cheese with a water. A woman came out of the back just as Annie's food was served. She had the same salt-and-pepper hair and thick, dark brows as the man at the grocery store. The two could be twins. She had to be Betty.

She gave Annie a hard look. Annie set her sandwich down, then ventured a glance toward the woman.

"Bernie called me," Betty said as she slipped into the seat across from her. "What restaurant experience do you have?"

4

"I've waited tables since I was sixteen."

Betty sent a look around her diner, which was half-full with only one other waitress working. "I can only pay the standard wages. You keep your tips, but folks around here aren't great tippers. I'd need you here an hour before we open to help prep for the day. And you'll need to stay an hour after closing to clean up. So that's five a.m. to three p.m."

Annie smiled. "I can do that."

Betty looked at her sandwich. "I do offer two meals a day, since the wages are shit. And you can take one day off during the week. Saturday, it's all hands on deck."

"Okay."

"When can you start?"

"Tomorrow morning."

"What's your name?"

"Annie Bergen."

"Well, Annie, I'm Betty Gifford. I guess you got yourself a job."

Annie wanted to jump across the table to hug her. She grinned at her sandwich instead, which wavered a bit before she blinked away her sudden tears. One big hurdle down. She could afford to stay at the motel a bit longer while she looked for other arrangements. Maybe someone in town had a room they could rent.

"You got a place to stay?" Betty asked.

Annie shook her head.

"My nephew has a cabin for rent down at the RV park just outside town. I can call him, if you like."

A job and a roof over her head. It was too good to be

true. Maybe she did have an angel. "I'd like that. If I can afford it."

"He won't gouge you. He'd have to answer to me." Betty grinned.

"Thanks, Betty. I appreciate it."

Annie finished her sandwich, paid for it, then, headed to the camp. It wasn't too far. She had to drive up out of the wide valley where the town was located. The campground was beautifully situated on a wide plateau that looked out over the village below. An ancient riverbed had carved its way through the sand-stone, forming the canyon. That river was now just a fast-running creek, but it kept the ravine green. The ravine was a stark contrast to the scrappy desert of the plateau, but all of it was rugged and stunning.

The campground seemed large, but maybe that was because it was barely occupied. She wondered how busy it would be in the summer season. Even with the town on its last legs, she had to think visitors would bring their recreational vehicles out to this hidden gem.

Right in the middle of the compound sat a small log cabin with a sign designating it as the office. Annie parked and went in to speak to the operator. He was a skinny guy, light brown hair—deeply involved in some-thing on his computer. He looked up, then frowned and came over to the counter.

"You Annie?"

"I am."

"Betty called. I'm Caleb." He put a set of keys on the counter. "Your cabin's over there." He pointed to the front corner of the campground. "Can't miss it. It's the middle one. Rent's two hundred a month. I got a master key if you get locked out. My cell's on the key tag."

Two hundred. So cheap. What if it was a rat hole? Filthy? "Um…"

"You got other options?" He laughed.

She blushed. No, he had her there. Didn't mean she didn't want to be sure it was a clean and safe place. "No. Does it leak? Is it clean?"

Caleb looked insulted. He grabbed the keys. "Let's go have a look."

They walked across the big campground, which gave Annie a chance to really check things out. The grounds were well tended. The drive was gravel, but the RV pads were concrete. She could see the cabin they were headed toward—a rustic log cabin, painted brown.

"How long you staying?" Caleb asked.

"I'm not really sure. Maybe a while. I just got a job at your aunt's diner."

At the cabin, they walked around to the backside, which faced a magnificent view overlooking the wide ravine between the bluff they were on and the opposite ridge. It was such a perfect spot that Annie felt it had to make up for any shortcomings in the cabin itself.

He unlocked the door and pulled it open. She stepped inside and drew a shocked breath. It was gorgeous. And absolutely perfect for her.

"Same key works on both the front and back doors."

Everything had been remodeled while preserving all the vintage charm. The fridge and stove were a matching teal. She wondered if they were original or just made to look retro. The windows were dressed in cottage-style curtains of white cotton with teal trim. The cabin was long and narrow, with a bedroom at one end, the living room at the other, and the kitchen in the middle. Separating the bedroom from the kitchen was a bathroom and a closet.

It was even nicer than her current hotel room. Her eyes watered as she looked back at Caleb. "You may never get me out of here."

He laughed. "My aunt thinks all I do is sit around and play video games. But this is what I want to do — restore vintage campers and cabins. My girlfriend did the design and sewing."

"You two have a magical skill. I can't believe I get to stay in a place like this. Maybe one day I can buy my own place and hire you to fix it up."

"We'd love to do that. I can even consult on whatever you're looking at."

"I'm sorry I doubted you." She handed him the cash, and he handed her the keys. "You sure it's only the two hundred a month?"

He looked about to say something, but then nodded. "We do have wildlife come through here. Don't leave your car unlocked; bears like to get in and root around for food. And bring your trash over to our bin — it's bear-proof."

Bears.

Scary as that sounded, the human animals who'd been trailing her were worse.

"It is safe here, right?"

"Yeah." He smiled. "Haven't lost a camper yet."

But had he ever had one with a stalker?

"You've been running this a while?"

"Just the past couple of years. Aunt Betty and Uncle Bernie own it. People really haven't discovered this place yet. That's another thing my girlfriend is working on. If we can make enough money running it, we're going to get married."

Annie smiled at him. "That's a great goal." She wished she used social media so she could help get word out, but that was dangerous behavior for her.

"Right. Well, if there's anything you need, you've got my number. I'll bring my girlfriend up to the diner so you two can meet."

"I'd like that. Thank you, Caleb."

He tapped his fingers to his forehead, as if tipping an invisible hat. "Oh—there's heat but no air conditioning. Even though it's November, it can still get warm here during the day, but I wouldn't recommend your leaving your windows open while you aren't at home."

"Because bears…"

"Right."

After he left, she checked her watch—if she hurried, she'd make the checkout time at the motel where she was staying in the next town over, saving herself paying for an extra night.

She couldn't stop smiling as she got into her Jeep.

Everything was going to work out just fine. The people here were friendly. Betty didn't seem to remember her. She could be safe here, and she could stay as long as she needed.

ANNIE SAT in her idling car at the western branch of the canyon at the far end of town. It was past four p.m., but it wouldn't be dark for another hour. She could drive through the valley and be back to town in half that time. Her doors were locked. She had a full tank of gas. Her tires were good. There was no reason she'd have to stop anywhere along the way. She didn't even have to turn down the roads that would lead her to the hell spot.

Baby steps.

Just drive through the valley.

She was stronger than what had happened to her. Stronger, perhaps, because of what had happened.

A cold sweat made her skin feel clammy. This would only get worse the longer she procrastinated. She'd come to Harmony Falls to finish what had begun here. She desperately wanted to start over, which she couldn't do while devils were still out there, destroying lives.

She touched her foot to the accelerator and crawled forward. The speed limit was low, and she wasn't driving anywhere near it. The road through the valley wasn't straight and it wasn't flat, but it was full of the shadows of death. Funny that the bluffs overlooking this valley were open to the sky, but in the depths of this ravine, it was like being smothered by a fist.

She didn't look to the left or to the right, just kept

her gaze pinned forward, taking a hand off the wheel now and then to wipe the tears from her face. She'd failed them, her brothers and sisters. She'd gotten out and left them behind.

By the time she drove out of the valley, daylight was slipping into night, and she was sobbing. She couldn't do this. She couldn't live with who she was.

She should never have come back.

2

Nash Thompson made the walk of shame through the corridors of his office building, his head held high and a manila envelope burning his hand. He felt like a traitor. He was leaving everything that comprised his life—his brothers, his trident, his future—just a month shy of hitting his twentieth-year milestone. Eighteen of those years were spent as a special warfare operator. He looked straight ahead as he walked away from his life. A million thoughts pounded through his mind, but he was too numb to feel...anything.

Leave.

That was his only mission now. Keep his shit together and walk away. Every step brought memories of missions, triumphs, and tragedies. Most vividly, Kato's return from a recent mission wounded. They'd gathered around him, keeping vigil after his surgery, a surgery that should never have happened.

Nash had started to ask questions about that. He'd gone to Kato's family, seeking answers they couldn't give him. He'd talked them into having a civilian autopsy done, the results of which had triggered an investigation, then an admission of error.

His command ordered him to move on. Move on. Move on.

He couldn't. And because he couldn't, he was out.

But not for insubordination. He'd been framed as a drug dealer. The drug test he'd taken had been corrupted. He was clean. Always had been. But the evidence was overwhelming against him, so his command had had to act.

His commanding officer had summoned him into a meeting, with all the lawyers present, and presented him with his other-than-honorable discharge, effective immediately. They told him to be grateful he wasn't going to be court-martialed.

But he might as well have been. He was a pariah now. He'd been stripped of his clearance. He'd never be able to work in security. He'd lost his pension. He'd lost all benefits due a vet. Nine tours to Afghanistan no longer had any meaning.

His whole fucking life.

He was going to have to start over, as if the last twenty years had never happened. And good luck getting a job. Every employer would do a background check.

He made it to his truck without any further

confrontations. The last thing he had to do was clear out of his base apartment. After that, it was over.

All of his belongings fit into a box and two suitcases. Twenty years of his life, and that was all he had to show for it. He considered packing his uniforms, but what the fuck for? The rest of his shit had come with the furnished apartment. He was just turning out lights when he heard a commotion in the hall outside his front door.

Motherfuckers. Couldn't leave well enough alone.

He yanked the door open. Four guys stood clustered there. His closest friends from the team. He glared at them, then stepped back and let them in. Holding up a hand, he made a show of taking his phone out of his pocket and setting it on the kitchen counter. The other guys did the same. He led them into the bedroom and shut the door.

"You shouldn't have come," Nash said.

"The fuck," Greyson said. "Like any of us believe what they're saying about you. We know you."

"The brass should have known you too," Borat said.

Nash shrugged. "I hit too close to the truth. They sold Kato's kidney. But since he was listed as an organ donor, and they'd legally harvested a lot from him after his death, no one caught it in the official autopsy. The thing is, because I was able to stop the cremation, his family's autopsy showed he was alive when one of his kidneys had been taken. And he couldn't have died from septicemia if his remaining organs were deemed viable. I know something's going on, but I couldn't prove who's behind it."

"What do we do?" Fish asked.

Nash looked at him, the newest member of the team. God, he resented having to leave them. "You have to hate me. To save yourselves, you disparage the shit out of me. Go with the storyline."

"What are you going to do?" Thiago asked.

"I'm going to keep digging."

"How, when you're out of the loop now?" Borat said.

"I was out of the loop before. I never could get medical records, but I can look at official reports and patch the pieces together."

"As if those haven't been doctored," Borat replied.

"True. But there may be patterns I can find. I need time to do that analysis."

Fish came close and held up a hand. Hooking thumbs with Nash, he pulled him into a hug. "You will always be one of us. Fuck shunning you. You need us, we're there."

"Thanks. Watch your sixes," Nash warned them. "Consider everything bugged, your entire digital footprint tracked. At least for a while. And for fuck's sake, if you ever take a blood or piss test, go that exact same day to a non-military doctor or outside lab and have the same tests done. I never thought they could set me up to fail the way they did."

With that critical convo over, they returned to Nash's living room and hit the case of beers the guys brought. For the next—painful—fifteen minutes, Nash endured a walk down memory lane. Soon his team would have new memories that he wasn't a part of. They'd go on being heroes while he went off in shame.

Greyson hooked an arm around his neck and pulled him close, growling in his ear, "You are and will always be a hero." Like he'd read Nash's mind or something.

"Sure." Nash tried to smile as he shoved his hands in his pockets. "You assholes need to leave. I'm heading out."

"We're goin'," Borat said. "But you're the asshole for dealing dope and getting yourself kicked out." He winked at Nash.

The others piped up with similar insults as they left.

The silence when they were gone was brutal. He'd never have that camaraderie again. That was what hurt the most. He brought his stuff out to the living room, then made a last pass around his apartment.

His doorbell rang.

Shit. He couldn't take more soul-wrecking goodbyes. He didn't rush to the door, but then felt like a coward for hiding. He crossed the living room and yanked his door open. No one was there. Just another manila envelope, but this one was thick.

Nash considered calling Borat back to have Fink check out the package, but he didn't. His apartment was on base, for fuck's sake. Who could get through so much security to attack him there?

Stupid question. Someone obviously had high-level access if they'd been able to set him up as they had.

He looked at the package. Maybe he had a death

wish. Maybe he hoped it was a bomb. Wouldn't surprise him that his enemies wanted him ended.

He broke the seal and dumped the contents on his coffee table. A phone and a wad of money. Make that a wad of Franklins. Had to be thousands of dollars there.

The phone rang. Geez, could this get weirder?

He picked it up but didn't speak.

"Nash Thompson?"

"That's me. Who's this?"

"You can call me Charley."

"Uh-huh. Why are we talking?"

"I have a job for you."

"Yeah? Get in line."

"I can help you."

"I don't want your help."

"Maybe not, but the people I'm sending you to need yours."

"Help with what?"

"You're working on an investigation, yes?"

"No. That crashed and burned like a fucking fireball."

"It's unlike you to give up when the fight's not over."

"You didn't hear me, lady? I've been burned. I'm done."

"No. You've been freed up for the next thing. The job I have for you overlaps your investigation. I need your help. My clients need your help. You can prevent more needless deaths."

"Look, I'm not in a frame of mind for mysteries. If

you know something, tell me. If you don't, I'm fucking hanging up."

The call dropped.

He tossed the phone on the couch, then glared at it, almost expecting it to ring again. He took his box out to his truck, then came back for his suitcases. He glanced at the cash and phone, then shook his head. That was a level of trouble he could do without. He was still on the base. If he was stopped with a wad of cash like that, his enemies would think it proved he was a dealer.

He wheeled his suitcases out of his apartment. He hadn't locked his place—he'd left the keys on the kitchen counter. He'd let the fucking Navy figure out what the hell to do with the contents of that package and everything else in his apartment. He was done.

He put his suitcases in the bed of his truck, then got inside. Taped to his dashboard was the name of a town: Harmony Falls, Colorado.

What. The. Fuck.

He wasn't interested. He had enough trouble in his life—he couldn't take on more. Besides, look where helping someone had gotten him. His whole life had been taken away.

Shit.

He got out of his truck and stomped back into his apartment. The phone and money were right where he'd left them. He grabbed both, then left—for good this time.

Guess he was headed to Harmony Falls, Colorado.

3

The fans hanging from tin tiles in the diner moved at different speeds. The restaurant was in a mid-century brick building. Looked as if it had recently undergone a significant remodel and modernization. Parts seemed new, and others were kitschy with western paraphernalia. He didn't know how much of the Old West decor was original or recently added, but it fit in this remote town.

He spotted a waitress going about her work. He watched her a moment, trying to see what made him notice her. It wasn't that her hands shook — her whole body did. Not violently, more like the high-pitched vibration of a mind on constant alert. Her eyes were restless, but she avoided eye contact. She moved in a silent way that was almost furtive, disturbing in her attempts to not be disturbing.

She took his order and left, tucking her order pad in

her apron pocket as she stopped at another table to grab what empty dishes she could manage.

She wasn't why he was here—she was just another pup mauled by life. He had to ignore her.

Why had Charley sent him here? The town was dead—or dying, anyway. The people in the diner were locals, old-timers too dug-in to move on. If their sun-bleached work clothes didn't give them away, their beater trucks did.

What kept them here?

But then, why not stay?

Nash had been all over the Middle East, Europe, across North, Central, and South America for a job he'd spent the last twenty years of his life on. Maybe one place was as good as another, if it was where you set your roots.

He'd done some research on Harmony Falls on his way out. The town had recently changed its name from Blanco Ridge, reinventing itself like a WITSEC recipient, hiding from its past. The cult that had owned the valley had been dissolved, most of its leaders jailed, but Nash had no doubt that some of the locals in the diner were still associated with the former polygamist society.

The waitress brought his order over. She had bleached blond hair and a smattering of freckles. She was thin, which made her eyes seem too big. God, those eyes. They were pale gray-blue, slightly darker than cave ice. For some reason, she looked right at him, met his eyes. He went still, holding his breath, shocked to be the recipient of her arctic gaze. He didn't look away, just let her take all that she could read in his eyes. The moment stretched into forever, but it was over too fast.

When she left, he realized his heart was beating loud enough for the people two tables over to hear.

You'll know it when you see it, Charley had said. Was this woman "it"?

What did she know that could be useful to him? And why had Charley sent him here, to Harmony Falls?

What am I looking for? he'd asked the stranger on the other end of the line when the second call came in while he was en route here.

You'll know it when you see it, she answered. *Your travel details are being messaged to you. Read it before it disappears.*

Those orders were to come to this hole in the wall and stay at the campground just outside town. That was it.

Nash finished his meal, then crossed the street to the town's grocery store. If Charley had set him up with a cabin, then she must be thinking he'd be here a while. Best grab some supplies.

The carts the store offered were miniature versions of those at regular groceries. Made sense, he supposed. The shop itself was small. The aisles were just wide enough for two of those tiny carts to pass. Charley had told him his cabin had been supplied with everything but fresh foods — milk, meat, veggies.

He picked out supplies for a couple of days, then went to the cashier.

The man was in his middle years and was slightly

rumpled. He began ringing up Nash's purchases. "You new here? Or just passing through?"

"Passing through."

"Planning on staying long?"

"Does it matter?"

"It might."

"Why?"

"Depends on why you're here."

"Seems like a nice place to decompress." Or it did before the inquisition. The guy gave him a hard look. Nash smiled. "You disagree? Seemed pretty quiet to me."

"It is quiet. We like it that way."

"Great. Then we have that in common. What do I owe you?"

"Thirty-eight ninety-five."

Nash laid out two twenties and waited for his change. Outside the front window, he saw an old Jeep pull into a space. The woman from the diner got out of it. Nash tried to ignore her, but the draw he felt toward her was too strong. His instincts were rarely wrong. He took his change and carried his bags, passing her on his way out.

She looked at him with those ice-laser eyes of hers. He felt time stop as he stared back at her. When she was behind him, freeing him of his momentary paralysis, he winced. What the hell was wrong with him? He was acting like a kid who'd just noticed women had curves.

He tossed his groceries in his truck's passenger seat, then backed out, reversing far enough that he could look at the girl's license plate. It was a temporary tag from Colorado, which didn't tell him much. He'd been curious to know if she was from the area or was an outsider. The grocery store clerk's friendly greeting to her said she was either from around there or had become a welcome addition to the town, possibly because of her job.

Maybe *he* needed a job—or at least a reason for being in town.

He drove to the RV park where his cabin was. This op had the framework of a long-term surveillance, not what he'd hoped for. He'd wanted a quick surgical strike against the bad guys harvesting organs. Instead, by letting Charley, an unknown commodity, call the shots, he was out here in bum-fuck nowhere, cooling his heels and pissing off the locals. Charley seemed to have the answers he was after, or she'd talked like she did. But how was that possible? He'd been digging into the medical crime ring for months, and the only thing he'd achieved was tanking his own career and being forced to abandon his brothers on the team.

Right now, Charley's cryptic snipe hunt was his best —his only—hope of taking his enemies down and getting his life back on track, so he had to see it through.

The cabin that his mysterious patron had provided was basically a studio, with a bed and bathroom at one end, then a galley kitchen, and a sofa at the other end. The decor embraced the rustic appeal of the log walls, using florals and buffalo plaids together, as if the patterns complemented each other.

He went to put his groceries away, cursing the fact

that he'd neglected to grab some beer. When he opened the fridge, a case of Budweiser sat on one of the shelves. He stared at it a moment, thinking that the dossier Charley had compiled on him was far too detailed.

He grabbed a can and went outside. The park had a row of cabins occupying premium spots right along a ridge overlooking a wide canyon that separated the park from the bluffs on the other side. It was pale dirt and green desert shrubs, raw and breathtaking. He hadn't lied to the guy at the store—this was a great place to unwind.

If only he'd come here for that purpose.

A car pulled up next door. That old Jeep. His girl got out. Well, not *his* girl, but his person of interest. She stopped short when she saw him. Didn't look too happy about it. He smiled and lifted his can in greeting. She ignored him and went into her cabin.

Nash took a swig of his Budweiser. The girl wasn't why he was here, but something about her tugged at him.

A moment later, she came back out. She paused beside her cabin, but then pulled her courage about her and came over to him. "Why—" She lifted her frosty eyes to look at him, then seemingly abandoned whatever it was that she was going to say. He frowned, waiting. She drew a ragged breath that seemed to catch in her throat. She tried to take another one, but the previous breath was still locked in her chest.

Did she have asthma?

He was about to reach for her, fearing she was going to pass out, but she hurried back to her cabin.

That was weird. Was she all right? He set his beer down and went over to her place. Her door was open, so he stepped inside. When she saw him, all color left her face. She held a hand out, as if to stop him as she struggled backward.

He followed her across the cabin, worried for her. She was having some kind of attack. "Hey. What's happening? You okay?"

She bumped into the dinette table, then scrambled sideways along her kitchen counter. "I don't want to die. Please."

Whoa. What the fuck?

Her statement was accompanied by breathing so rapid that none of it seemed to hit her lungs. She was struggling for air. She was hyperventilating.

Why?

What about him had set her off?

He did a quick look around her place, trying to find something he could use to help her calm down. There was a white paper bag on the counter. He grabbed it and emptied it, then brought it over to her. Her cabin had the same shotgun setup as his. He didn't like that she kept backing up to the bed. She was likely to feel worse if he kept coming toward her, but it was his fault that she was like this, and he was the only one here to help.

"Easy." He held up a hand. He had no idea if breathing into the bag was really a thing, but if it worked as a distraction from her panicked state, then it would serve its purpose.

She cringed as if waiting for a blow.

He opened the bag and crumpled the top. "Hold this to your mouth." He pushed the bag toward her. "Yeah. Breathe into it." She looked skeptical. "Just do it."

The back of her legs hit the edge of the bed. She sat down. Nash kneeled in front of her, his hands on her knees as he watched to see if the old trick with the bag worked. Her iceberg eyes never left his. After a moment, her breathing did settle back into something more normal. She lowered the bag, but then her eyes dropped to his hands on her legs. He pulled them away fast, then stood and backed away.

"Jesus, you scared me." He sat on one of the dinette seats. "What just happened?"

"Are you going to kill me?"

"Um... No?"

"I've seen you before."

"I doubt that. I would seriously never forget you. I'm Nash Thompson."

She rubbed her forehead, but didn't respond in kind —maybe because the nametag she still wore labeled her as Annie. "You can go now."

"Right. Well, I'm just next door if you need me." He paused. What if she was wearing a borrowed nametag? "I didn't catch your name."

She glared at him. "You know who I am."

He shook his head. "You've got me confused with

someone else. I sure as hell never meant to scare you."
He saw himself out.

The meds he'd dumped out of the prescription bag
were for anxiety. What was up with her? She was terrified of something. He'd triggered a fear so deep that it
had nearly shredded her on its way out.

You'll know it when you see it. Charley's words drifted
through his mind again. Maybe he would. Then again,
maybe he wouldn't even if it bit him.

What the hell kind of mission objective was that
vague?

ANNIE HURRIED to lock the door. It wouldn't deter
someone determined to get inside, but it made her feel
safer. They'd never talked to her before. The men
tracking her had always kept their distance, sometimes
making themselves known simply by crossing paths with
her or loitering near her. Whenever that happened, she'd
leave town. Avoiding them had never been much of a
plan—it had certainly never worked for very long,
which was why she'd come back here.

She hadn't even begun what she'd come to do. She
wasn't leaving until she had proof.

She looked out the window, trying to gauge how far
she'd have to run to get into her Jeep. Would he catch
her? Did he not kill her just now because it would be
harder to hide the evidence? Was she safer staying
where she was, or should she make a break for it?

She looked at her key ring on the counter. There was a key to the diner on it. She could sleep on the couch in the office and see how she felt about things in the morning. She just had to wait for the sun to go down so he wouldn't see her leave. Her stuff was already packed — she always kept herself ready to run. That was something she'd learned soon after leaving foster care.

If she crashed on the couch in Betty's office, she was going to have to explain why. She'd have to come up with a lie the older woman would believe. The fewer people who remembered her, the better. Betty had helped her way back then, but Annie wasn't certain if the older woman remembered her. The complaint she'd made fourteen years ago had been a big deal at the time, shocking the townsfolk. But after several interviews and a field trip out to the site, when none of her assertions could be proved, Annie had become a liar and an attention seeker to everyone except Betty. The whole thing quietly died.

She wished she had, too.

She clasped her plastic trash bag close and sat on the dinette seat, waiting for darkness. She knew how to be still and quiet. She could do that for hours.

At last, darkness filled her cabin and the world around them. She peeked through one of the windows over at the guy's cabin. His lights were on. She couldn't quite tell where he was, but she watched until she saw him move, a silhouette in the room's warm light.

He was somewhere in the middle of his cabin. She could slip out and get into her Jeep before he could get to her. She picked up her bag. Her door creaked when she opened it. Best move quickly now. She closed it and started toward her Jeep, then realized she couldn't leave her cabin unlocked. God alone knew what would be waiting for her when she returned—if she returned. She dashed back to lock the cabin door then hurried to her car, painfully aware of the gravel crunching under each step. She unlocked her Jeep and got inside, quickly locking the door. With another look around, she started her car and backed up slowly. She wanted to go fast, just peel out of there, but there was still a possibility that she could slip away without having him follow her.

Worried another panic attack might start while she was driving, she forced herself to keep her breathing calm as she watched the road ahead and behind, watched the waysides left and right.

They wouldn't just kill her if they caught her. They'd carve her up and sell her for parts.

They'd done that to her friends.

And no one had believed her, not the cops, not her foster families.

She was going to die here, but at least the truth would come out.

4

Annie heard someone fit a key into the lock at the diner's back entrance. She'd been wakeful and on alert the whole night, the same as any night. She had her jacket draped in front of her, her bag at her feet. She knew she should have a story already prepared, but hadn't come up with any. Hopefully, Betty wasn't angry.

But it wasn't Betty who stopped in the hallway—it was Gus, the cook. Relief washed through Annie.

"What are you doing here?" he asked.

She shrugged. "I sort of had a problem at my cabin."

Gus frowned. "What happened?"

"A new guy took the cabin near mine. It got weird."
I got weird, she corrected herself, but stopped short of fessing up to Gus.

"What did he look like?"

"White guy. Tall. Light brown hair. Blue eyes. I dunno."

"Yeah, I saw him. Want me to talk to him? What did he do that sent you running here?"

"Nothing. He was friendly. I just panicked." She stood and grabbed her stuff. She'd change in the ladies' room. "Look, could you maybe not say anything to Betty?"

"No problem. I've crashed here myself from time to time."

GAVIN ERICKSON HATED THIS TOWN, but he'd loved being its police chief back in the day. When everything went down with the Society, it was his cooperation with the FBI that had let him dodge any charges. Though being a member of the Grummond Society had been mandatory for everyone employed by the cult, he'd never subscribed to its beliefs, just its benefits.

Now, all the same shit was starting up again.

"We thought you had this handled," Crash said to Gavin. The guy was one of Travis' enforcers.

"I do. I will. I'm taking care of it." Gavin gestured with his hand, brushing the implied threat aside. Goddamn, he hated the shakedown. He'd deal with the girl. It was a longstanding promise he made himself; her return would be her death. It just so happened that these thugs wanted her demise even more than he did. The fuck of it all was that they needed her alive.

She knew things. And she was back. Most of the town's residents had moved away, so it wasn't like her return would cause much of a ripple. Besides, she'd just been a kid then. He'd done a good job scrubbing his involvement in the crazy story she'd come to town with fourteen years ago. He couldn't make her disappear then, but he contained her story by twisting her report of what was going on at that house outside of town into the demented concoction of a teenage runaway. And he had been able to speed her transference into the care of social services, getting her out of town quickly, before someone, like that do-gooder Betty, decided to foster the girl.

"Whatever you do, don't kill her," Travis, the gang's leader, said. "She's worth a two-million-dollar payday for us."

"You gonna do the deed here, in this dump?" Gavin asked.

"Doc's got it under control," Travis said. "His crew can put a surgical site together in no time. They've done that for customers in the Middle East and South America. As for the rest of the medical center, he'll decide after this project if he wants to make it a permanent thing. That ain't our business. Our job is to make sure everything goes smoothly. We want our payday too."

Yeah. Same for Gavin—and his freedom, which they'd promised if he handled the acquisition of the donor.

All right, already. He'd get it done. But it would be on his terms.

NASH PARKED down the street from the diner the next morning. Given the suspicious way the clerk at the grocery store reacted to him yesterday and the scarcity of outsiders in town, he couldn't successfully pass himself off as a tourist. No casual traveler he knew would stay long in a semi-hostile place like this.

And why was it hostile, anyway?

Whatever. He needed a reason to explain why he was in town. Maybe he'd come up with one while he ate.

He took a seat in the same booth he'd used yesterday, hoping it was in Annie's section. She saw him and brought over a coffee pot and filled his mug. Her hand was almost steady. "Morning."

"Howdy." Nash nodded. The woman was skittish as hell, so he didn't strike up a convo with her. Something about her screamed at him to just stay inside the lines. He was a pro at that. He'd spent a career on that narrow track…until his friend died.

"Ready to order?" she asked when she came back to refill his mug.

"What's the special?" He knew, because he'd read the chalkboard on his way in, but the question gave him the opportunity to hear her voice for a few extra moments. Really, what was it about her that fascinated him so? She wasn't a natural blond; her long, bleached hair was growing out, revealing a cap of dark auburn hair. He liked the freckles that were sprinkled across her nose and cheeks.

"Any of that sound good?" she asked, a little irritated.

"Yeah. All of it. I'll go for the breakfast burrito with green chili."

She nodded and pivoted away.

He drew a shaky breath. Maybe the thing about her that fascinated him wasn't her at all but the dragons shadowing her. What would bring a girl like her to a place like this? Was she running from something? Hiding from a stalkerish ex?

He sipped his coffee, reminding himself not to get distracted from his mission. She wasn't why he was here.

Three men came into the diner. Nash recognized two from the day before. They sat in Annie's section. She treated them as cordially as she did Nash. Poured their coffees. Took their orders. Made as little eye contact as possible. When she turned to go, one of them grabbed her wrist, stopping her. Startled, she cried out. Coffee sloshed from the glass pot.

The man chuckled. "Bring me some milk, sweetheart."

She yanked her hand free. Her sneakers carried the wet coffee across the floor. Nash glared at the back of the guy's head, fantasizing about a dozen different ways he could kill him. He tore his gaze away and forced a calming breath to ease his flash of anger. He didn't know if Annie was involved in what he was here to do, so he had to keep a low profile at the moment.

Annie brought his food. He nodded at her. She seemed relieved he didn't want to chat. He took his time eating, intending to wait out the fools who'd felt free to touch her. When they left, he went to the front counter to pay his bill. The men got into a Land Rover. He texted himself the license plate, knowing Charley would see it.

"How was your breakfast?" a middle-aged woman in an apron asked. Her nametag read, "Betty."

"Great." He handed her some cash.

The woman sized him up and didn't look pleased. "With all due respect, I don't think you should hang around in town."

"Why's that?"

"'Cause you look like you're passing through, and you should just get that done."

Nash gave a little shrug. Time for his cover story. "I might be looking for a job. You hiring?"

The woman looked down the counter to Annie, who seemed frozen in place. Fear. More goddamned fear. "I could use another hand, but I'm not sure you're the one."

"Hire me until you find the person you're looking for."

"Why do you want to work here?"

"I'm thinking of writing an article about the town. Working here might be a good way to meet folks."

The woman sighed, waved him back behind the counter, and disappeared into a hallway. He followed her past the kitchen and a storeroom into an office. She leaned against her desk. There were stacks of papers on the floor and desk and file cabinets. Her chair was a little frayed.

"You wouldn't like the job."

"I've done a lot of jobs I didn't like."

"It's a flex position. Some days you'll be a dish-washer. Some days a handyman. Some days a cook. Some days a delivery guy. Some days all of that."

"Works for me."

"You ever cook before?"

"I live alone, so yeah."

"You live alone, but you eat at a diner."

Nash smiled. "Didn't say I liked my cooking."

"How long do you plan on being in the area?"

"Don't know yet."

Betty stared at him. Narrowing her eyes, she seemed to make up her mind, and not in his favor. "Where did you come from? Where did you last work?"

Nash shoved his hands in his pockets. First rule of lying was to keep it close to the truth. "I just left the Navy. Under an other-than-honorable release."

"They kicked you out."

"Yeah."

"Why?"

"Fighting."

"Why were you fighting?"

"It's what they trained me to do."

"Huh. I don't take no nonsense here. I don't think I need your kind of trouble here. I'm gonna pass."

"Got it. Thanks for the chat." Great. He couldn't even land a job as a flex worker. What the fuck was he going to do if this investigation didn't work and he couldn't get his life back?

"Oh—and one more thing. Leave Annie alone. She should be able to sleep in her own cabin in peace."

"I agree. I didn't know that she didn't."

He almost ran into Annie in the short hallway. Her eyes locked with his. He tried to read everything those pale orbs were saying but couldn't, so he just gave her a nod as he passed her. Even the cook gave him a glare as Nash went past the storage room. What had Annie said about him to all of them?

He walked out of the diner, feeling heavy. Something was not right in this town.

Harmony Falls was not very harmonious.

He was on his way back to the campground when a text came through. No identifying number. He read it on his dash's screen. *Well done.* He didn't respond, but the validation helped him know he was on the right track—whatever that meant in this case. Charley was congratulating him for failing a job interview. Made no sense, any of this, but he had to stick it out. He owed Kato that much, at least. His own life was fucked, but he'd be damned if he let his friend die in vain, a terrible, needless death, harvested by monsters when he couldn't fight back.

Nash drove around Harmony Falls. It was nearly a ghost town. Judging from the many empty homes and businesses, it had been much more densely populated at one time. He supposed the town had grown up around the cult, and once that organization was broken up, the town lost its way. It certainly lost its people.

After a while, he went back to his cabin to reset and

make a plan. He'd just taken a beer from his fridge when he heard a car move down the gravel drive. Was Annie back? His gut said whatever was going on here had something to do with her.

It wasn't Annie's Jeep that came in. He watched to see which site the car was going to. It parked at Annie's. She was still at work, so who was visiting? Two men got out and walked around her cabin, looking at his as they passed between them. They pounded on her door. Both men went back to the car and drove off again.

He looked at his phone, wondering how involved Charley was in this little job she'd given him. "You got eyes on my place, Charley?" he said to no one in particular. Charley had been listening the whole time he'd been talking to Betty, so he was pretty sure she could hear him now.

Yes, came a texted response.

"You got eyes on Annie's?"

Yes. Those men will kill her if she doesn't back down.

"Well, fuck. It. All. An answer—half an answer, anyway. That wasn't hard, was it?"

Keep her safe. She's an important witness.

"That's the plan."

Don't go digging into them—we know who they are. I've sent partial dossiers to your email.

"Then what's my role in all of this? I'm not a U.S. marshal." Or a babysitter.

Follow the leads. See where they take you. I need you to corroborate—or invalidate—our findings.

"And what are your findings?"

Senator Whiddon, who died a while back, was secretly deeply involved in the Grummond Society. He used his government position to make connections with international crime syndicates, including a ring of organ traffickers in the Middle East. That relationship between Harmony Falls and the traffickers outlived the senator. We don't know how. The chatter we've intercepted points to a transaction happening soon. That's why I said you'll know it when you see it. Keep your eyes open. Annie is after proof. Help her get it. Tread lightly. There are power players involved in this who can make it disappear, as they've been doing for more than a decade. The difference now is that we have Annie. And you. I want whoever's involved taken alive, Nash.

"Copy that." He sipped his beer. At least his instincts were still intact—he'd been right about Annie being involved in all of this.

5

Nash was a door kicker, not an analyst. Research and analysis were handled by the intelligence officers on his ops, but he didn't have that kind of support at the moment, so he had to go it alone. What was it that made Charley think there was a connection between his traffickers and this town? The cabin had come with a laptop and a VPN, letting him surf without anyone here sniffing him out. He spent the rest of that afternoon reading everything he could find online about the Grummond Society, its leaders, lieutenants, adherents, victims, and apostates. It was a lot to go through, but there were big holes in the info he was finding.

Taking a break from his research, he opened the dossiers for the guys from the diner. Their rap sheets included extortion, loan sharking, enforcers for crime lords, sex trafficking, and murder. A town like Harmony Falls could hold little appeal to thugs like that, but something had brought them here. What that was didn't much matter; wherever they went, trouble followed. The things on their records were the same types of crimes as those that had taken down the Grummond Society's leadership.

Were they connected to the town's incarcerated leaders?

No wonder Betty and Bernie had been so standoffish. The cook hadn't been thrilled with him either. Nor was Annie. What did they know?

He heard a car pull up and park in front of Annie's cabin. She was home from her shift. He watched her take a trash bag out of her Jeep and head inside. He wondered if those guys who'd come by earlier had left something for her, but she didn't rush back out. A few moments later, she came out the back door with a laptop, a bottle of water, and a jump rope. She'd changed into workout clothes. She did some stretches, then used the jump rope for a period of time. Then she did some tai chi. Lastly, she fired up a video and went through several exercises that looked like some version of martial arts. Krav Maga, maybe.

Her movements were fluid, more like dance steps than martial arts. She was posturing, like a person who'd never fought or actually sparred with anyone. Did she do this every day? Was she training for something or just exercising? She clearly had been doing this a while; she hadn't needed to look up the steps of her tai chi workout. And her first few exercises with Krav Maga were well practiced.

He wanted to get out there and spar with her, but he doubted her reaction to that would be any more welcoming than any of their previous interactions.

He needed to find a way to learn more about the town. He doubted there was a library—Harmony Falls had only recently been properly incorporated, so it was still getting established with the regular social services. Besides, access to secular knowledge wasn't something permitted by elders while the cult had owned the town. That didn't mean there wasn't some of the documentation he was looking for; he just had to find the person or people who kept that history.

Perhaps he should start with the one local he had some kind of rapport with—Betty, the diner owner, if two meals and a failed job interview made a relationship, that was.

NASH ENTERED the diner at the tail end of the lunch hour the next day, timing it so he would be one of the last customers to leave. As always, he sat in Annie's section. Her manner was as cold as her eyes. She was the unfriendliest human he'd ever met. Not that it mattered. He wasn't here to make friends. And the information he was after would likely tear apart what was left of this town.

He ordered a Cobb salad and an ice water and took his time eating when his meal came. Table by table, the other diners finished and paid for their meals. Annie and another waitress began their daily cleanup tasks. Nash finished up. Betty came to the register to ring him up.

"Out of curiosity," Nash said, "is there a town historian still around?"

Betty glared at him. "Really, what's your interest in the town?"

"I mentioned that article I wanted to write. It's a human-interest piece."

"Well, don't write it about us."

"Why's that?"

"People who get nosy end up in the cemetery."

Whoa. Not the answer he was expecting. "Huh." He gave her a slight smile. "Now I want to do it even more. This town is reinventing itself. People everywhere are doing that, too—including me. Businesses are as well. Things are changing. It's an interesting process to document."

"We aren't bugs for you to study. And if you start asking questions, you can skip coming here. I don't want trouble." She gave him a hard look. "I knew you didn't want a job. You just wanted to spy on us for your article."

"I didn't hide that from you. The best way to get to know a place is to live in it, become a local. No better way to do that than to take a job where I can meet lots of people. Besides, why the need to protect the town's old secrets?"

Betty closed the cash drawer with a bang. "Maybe you should go talk to the mayor. She might have info that could help you."

"Thanks. I will."

His research had indicated that a new mayor had been elected recently, one of the longtime residents. She was still in a polygamous marriage but very much in favor of the town's modernization. She was an insider bringing outside values in—something that caused a fair amount of tension among some of the remaining long-term residents.

The small municipal center was located inside a house. He stepped inside and found a front counter with a few desks behind it. A bell on the door announced his arrival. As he stepped up to the counter, he saw a woman look up from her seat at a desk.

"Can I help you?" she asked.

"Yes. I'd like to make an appointment to speak to the mayor."

She smiled and stood. "You're talking to her. What can I do for you?"

"I'm thinking of writing a human-interest piece on Harmony Falls. I'm here to do some research."

"Betty called me. But why here? Why us?"

"Because, as I mentioned to Betty, it isn't very often that a town remakes itself. I'd like to learn more about that process. Maybe by talking to some original residents, or a town historian?"

"I bet Betty wasn't fond of your idea."

"She wasn't."

"You understand our town has been through a lot." The mayor came over and set her hands on her side of the counter. "Are you here to judge us?"

"No. Not at all. I'm fascinated in renewal and rein-venting oneself. It's something I'm having to do, too—I'm just out of the military. Life as a civilian after twenty years isn't easy. Harmony Falls is a beautiful place. I'd like to see it succeed."

The mayor held out her hand. "I'm Ester Sullivan."

Nash shook with her. "Nash Thompson. Nice to meet you. I was hoping I could at least start by reading old newspapers."

"I have most of those. You're welcome to have a look through them, but I do ask that they stay here."

"That would be great. But don't tell Betty. She offered to put me in a grave if I dug into the town."

Mayor Sullivan laughed. "She and her brother couldn't be more curmudgeonly if they tried. But they are good people. It's just that their world—ours, here in town—has changed rapidly since the Society broke up and our leaders went to jail."

"I guess so."

She lifted the drop shelf, inviting him back. "You can help me retrieve the binders. They're heavy."

He followed her to a closet that had been converted to a makeshift library. Shelves lined three walls with binders, papers, boxes—everything he was looking for.

"Any particular year you want to start with?"

"I need all of it. But let's begin with your earliest archives."

"Good choice. You can start with these newspapers from the 1940s. That's when the town really began. Prior to that, it was simply the community compound.

I've got the binders organized by decade. You're welcome to spend time here, but I do lock up between four and five p.m."

"This is terrific. I may need a few days here. Kick me out when you're ready to close for the night. What time do you open?"

"I'll be here at ten in the morning."

She left, and Nash took the oldest notebooks to the front office. For the next few hours, he lost himself in the lives of people who'd lived there eighty-some years earlier, just after the Second World War. Change had come to the town then, too. The young men hadn't been able to escape the draft. They'd been forced to get out in the world and then brought it home with them. There was a clash between those who wanted to keep the community closed and those who wanted to open it up, letting it grow and join the modern world—something that had taken it eighty years to start doing.

But what was most interesting about those early years was the secret infrastructure being put in place. Prior to the war, its isolation had been natural protection. After the war, as people and the country changed, becoming more mobile, the cult bought land surrounding its community, buying space to keep it insulated from the outside world, even as it adopted ever more egregious rules. What had begun as a benign utopian community late in the nineteenth century morphed into a cult that hungered for power over those in its small community.

That was as far as Nash got in his reading that afternoon. Those were his inferences, anyway. The town at the time didn't seem to be aware of the rights and privileges it was surrendering to its leadership—not that anyone was given a choice in the matter.

He was deep in thought as he left. Secret societies had free rein to practice any behaviors they wished, without oversight or management from outside forces. It was this dark construct that had let opportunists take advantage of the town's naiveté. Nash knew what had led to the government coming in and ripping it apart—sexual abuses, forced labor, murder, tax evasion, money laundering. It was a cesspit of human immorality.

How much of that was left? And who was left who would know the answers he was looking for?

What else did this town shield?

IT WAS TIME.

Annie couldn't put this off any longer. Thinking of what she had to do was keeping her up at night, making her jumpy and paranoid. The group of men who had been in the diner the last few days made her nervous. They looked at her as if they knew her. She hadn't seen them before, but her stalkers weren't always the same people.

She needed to get the evidence she was after. She would go after work.

She kept to herself the whole day. Betty and Nash both tried to draw her into conversations, but she didn't fall for it. She probably wasn't going to be staying here very long, after all. No point making friends with Betty. And she didn't for a minute believe Nash's nice-guy act. He was charming and friendly, playing the exact role needed to get through her protective walls.

That afternoon, she got home before Nash. Taking advantage of his absence, she scrambled to get her car loaded with her things, some food and water, her sleeping bag, and a flashlight. It was already getting dark when she locked her cabin and left the campground. Nash still wasn't home, which was a good thing. He had way more curiosity than any stranger should have.

She drove out of town, heading along the wide draw between the two ridges that could be seen from the campground. The ravine was a ten-mile stretch of river watershed that now was home to tall cottonwoods, aspen, willows, and pines—woods that were becoming skeletal versions of their summer selves. She went slower and slower, then stopped. She felt sick at the thought of where she was going.

This was stupid. Coming back to Harmony Falls had been a terrible idea. She had thought returning to where it all began would finally let her reset, begin again differently. Pretending it all hadn't happened hadn't helped her heal. Instead, it was a constant fight to suppress those memories, which kept her in a loop of bad experiences.

She wanted out of her hell.

A counselor had suggested letting herself relive those

days, acknowledge the terror and agony, letting those negative memories and emotions move through her so that she no longer had to fight them.

The best way to do that, Annie had decided, was to come back and find the evidence she needed to prove what had happened here—even if it meant confronting her stalkers.

And now that she was here, she wanted to vomit. She couldn't do this. Not now, not ever.

She turned around and left the woods that were so haunted with what had been.

OVER THE WEEK Nash had been in town, he made a point of eating at the diner once each day. For one, he got to see Annie. For two, he could keep an eye on how the locals were responding to the news that he was there digging around. And for three, he got to eat food he didn't cook himself.

He hadn't seen the three guys in the Land Rover again, but it seemed they might have a role in whatever was happening here.

Betty came over to refill Nash's coffee. "You enjoying digging your own grave?" she asked.

"I've been digging my grave since I was eighteen. Haven't been put in it yet."

"Are you finding what you're looking for?"

"Maybe. I hear you're holding out on me."

"I'm not the town historian. I'm a self-appointed

keeper of certain records. There's a difference." She sat across from him. Nash noticed she'd waited to come talk to him until the restaurant only had one other patron. "I'm sorry for stonewalling you."

Nash scoffed. "No, you're not."

"True." Betty shrugged. "It's just that we've been bombarded with the morbidly curious wanting to sensationalize what happened here, pulling out the nasty bits —which, I will grant, are many—but ignoring the fact that we're human, and we're survivors, and we're trying to put our lives back together."

"I get that. I can see it could be insulting." He wondered what she meant by the nasty bits. What did she know that might be a lead?

"Mayor Sullivan says you're good people."

Nash grinned. "I coulda told you that."

"I guess, when you're finished with the newspapers, you can come see me about other documents."

"Thank you, Betty. That's a huge help."

"But I'm still going to suggest that you get over to the cemetery." She leaned closer across the table and whispered, "Not all graves have markers—or are even in the cemetery."

Nash was shocked by that revelation. He looked up and caught Annie's stricken glance. It was almost as if she knew what Betty was talking about. How was that possible? She was as new in town as Nash. He'd learned that much, at least.

THE DAY'S LAST CUSTOMER, besides Nash, was standing at the cash register. Annie had seen him come in a few times over the last month but hadn't yet waited on him. She took his ticket. "Did you enjoy your lunch?" she asked as she rang him up.

"I did. You're new here."

Annie nodded.

"I'm considering opening a practice in town." The guy thrust his hand toward her.

Again, Annie nodded. "Nice to meet you." She put his change in his outstretched hand and shut the register.

Betty appeared out of nowhere to stand behind her. She greeted the doctor. Annie assumed that meant she was no longer needed, and slipped away from the conversation to go bus the doctor's table.

Why she got freaked out by the friendly doctor, she didn't know. He had a pleasant enough demeanor. Maybe it was just having a member of the medical profession here, in the town near where the kid farm was, that made her jumpy.

She put dishes in the bucket with a little more force than was needed. She was grown now. She never had to go see another doctor for the rest of her life. Never. It was her choice. She had that freedom.

She thought about Nash. He was another man to be wary of. He was entirely too observant. She hoped she'd been mistaken about his being one of the guys she'd seen tracking her over the years. He stood out in a crowd in a way the others didn't. They were more average in height and less fit.

Less striking.

She wondered, though, if panic was always going to be her reaction to meeting men.

"You good?" Nash asked.

She jumped, so lost in her thoughts that she hadn't noticed he was finished eating. She nodded, then lifted the dish bucket and would have left, but he blocked her.

"Have you ever seen him before?" He nodded toward the doctor at the register.

"Just in here."

NASH POCKETED HIS PHONE. He'd snagged a photo of the doctor, curious to see if Charley recognized him. Nash handed Betty his ticket and some cash at the register. "I overheard you're a doctor." Nash shook hands with the guy as he introduced himself.

"I'm Dr. Mason," the guy said. "This little town is growing fast. I'm thinking of a post-retirement career, maybe in a small town like this." He looked at Nash. "You new here too?"

Nash caught Betty's distrustful expression. He took his change. "Oh, don't count me in the town's growth," he said to the man. "I'm just passing through."

"Nash is writing an article on the town," Betty said.

"Ah. It does have an interesting past," the doctor said.

"It's not the past that I'm interested in. It's the town's present and how it's reinventing itself. Hey—if you do decide to come back and settle in, I'd love to interview you. It's a big deal getting a doctor to take up a practice here. Businesses like yours are the cornerstone of a town's revitalization."

Dr. Mason nodded. "Sure. If I do, come talk to me." He handed his card to Nash.

"Great. Thanks."

6

A few days later, Nash had time on his hands. Mayor Sullivan had to close the office for the day so that she could do something with her family. Nash headed back to the cabins. Annie hadn't been at the diner. It wasn't fair for him to expect to see her every day, but he did.

Caleb and his girlfriend, Ruby MacDonald, were walking out of Annie's place when Nash got back to the campground. Annie was with them. They were carrying blankets and bags of things to her Jeep. He waved to them as he headed to his cabin.

"Hey, Nash!" Caleb called out. "Want to come with us? We're heading up to the falls."

Nash looked at Annie. She was clutching her blanket and staring at the ground. A good guy would decline, but he wasn't feeling very charitable. "I'd love to. I've been wondering where the inspiration for the town's new name came from. I'll follow you out."

The place they were headed was a half-hour drive out of town, toward the western bluffs that overlooked the canyon. They parked in a gravel pull-off. Caleb opened the back hatch and grabbed a few things. Ruby did the same, leaving some food, two chairs, and a couple of blankets for Nash and Annie.

"I hope you don't mind my joining you," Nash said. Annie took the blanket he handed her and held it tightly as her eyes slowly moved up to meet his. He loved it when she looked at him, really looked at him, as if she were trying to discover something she only trusted his eyes to say. When her gaze lowered to his mouth, a warm hum started to buzz in his head.

"It's okay," she said.

He took that as a win. After grabbing the two chairs and her bag of food, he stepped back so she could lock her Jeep. It was a manual thing, so she had to go around to all the doors too.

"C'mon you two!" Ruby called out. They'd already made it a good way up the trail.

It was a beautiful day for a hike. Although it was early November, the weather was sunny and mild. Fifteen minutes further down the trail, the roar of distant water filled the air. The trail widened, opening to a big area of bare dirt. Someone had brought in a wooden picnic table. The waterfall was louder there. Nash set his things down and went to go have a look at the town's inspiration.

It was breathtaking. A hundred-foot drop from the top of the bluff, straight down to a little cove. Looked like a great place to go for a swim when the weather was warmer. The vegetation was thick where the water spilled out of the pool and moved downstream. The aspen were past their prime, but there was still plenty of yellow mixed in with the brown leaves. The willows were still green, though faded. The pines around them were still a deep green. It smelled fresh in that spot—a mix of peaty ground, water, pine needles, and sunshine.

"What do you think of our Milstone Falls?" Caleb asked.

"This should be a national park," Nash said.

"It's one of the reasons we wanted to rename our town. Tourists love waterfalls. Every year, we have people who come through to visit this one and check it off their list of obscure ones to visit."

Ruby joined them. "It's part of our rebranding. We'd like to become known for our beautiful landscape instead of our twisted history."

Nash looked beyond them to where Annie was sitting nearby, perched on a big granite boulder. He smiled at her. She didn't return the gesture—but she didn't look away, either.

"I'm going to get lunch started," Ruby said. "You hungry, Nash?"

"I'm not. You guys grabbed me right after a trip to the diner. But I'm glad to help."

At the picnic table, Ruby looked back toward the end of the trail where Annie was still sitting. "She's a quiet one."

Nash followed her gaze. "I don't think so. I've never

met anyone with so much noise in her head. This is good for her. It's peaceful here."

"It is. You guys make a great couple."

Nash huffed a laugh. "We're not together."

"No? You have so much chemistry."

"Really? We just met."

"Caleb and I hit it off right away." She leaned forward and spoke in a conspiratorial voice. "He's going to propose to me soon, I know it."

Nash smiled. "Excellent. That's great news."

Caleb joined them. He grabbed a pickle. "How's your research going for your article?"

"Betty tell you I was working on that?"

"Yep. Things don't stay quiet around here. Ours is such a small town that gossip makes its way around the whole place in about a half-hour. Plus, we don't get a lot of visitors staying in town, so we're naturally curious."

"Nosy, you mean," Ruby said.

"I'd be curious too," Nash said. "It's a lot of research. At the moment, I'm just going through Mayor Sullivan's archives. It's going to take me a while."

"She's got some ledgers that might interest you," Caleb said. "Births and deaths were recorded, as well as crimes and punishments. You'd get a kick going through them."

"Good to know. I'll be sure to ask for them."

Annie joined them. Ruby had the food situated on the picnic table. Nash took a bottle of water as the three of them ate their sandwiches and munched on the salad Annie had made. She was smiling as she watched Caleb and Ruby banter. Nash couldn't remember ever seeing her face relax.

Maybe they could come out here a few more times before the winter set in—or even after. He thought the snow on the evergreens and a half-frozen waterfall would be stunning.

Caleb's phone buzzed an alert. Nash checked his phone but had no reception. How was Caleb getting service?

"Oh, shoot. I forgot we have a new camper coming in this afternoon." Caleb looked at the group. "Glad I set an alarm. I hate to cut this short, but we do have to get back."

Annie looked sad but covered that up fast.

"Why don't you take my truck back?" Nash suggested. "I'll come back with Annie in a bit."

"You don't mind?" Caleb asked.

"Not at all."

"You good with that, Annie?"

She nodded.

"Great. Thanks. We'll haul some of this stuff out of here so you don't have to make two trips. See you back at the campground," Caleb said.

When they were alone, Annie gathered the remaining things into a pile. "There are cookies," she said.

"Did you make them?" Nash asked as he took one.

"No. I don't cook much. I got them from the diner."

"Mmm. Betty has a talent for making cookies." He looked around. "We could do a hike, if you wanted."

"What I really want is to sit quietly by the fall and just listen."

"Let's do that."

They went back to the fall and picked different rocks. Nash was turned just a bit so that he could check Annie now and then. He leaned back and shut his eyes, letting the roar of the water fill him. This could easily become a place of his heart.

He sat that way a while but was startled from his reverie by the unpleasant feeling of being watched. The water was so loud that anyone could sneak up on them. He'd really let his guard down. He looked over at Annie, only to find she was standing on her rock, looking back the way they'd come.

He went over and gave her a hand down. She was a big target standing there like that. Better put some trees between her and whatever it was they'd felt. Her eyes showed she was scared again.

"Did you hear something?" he asked.

"No. I didn't see anything either. It's just…a feeling."

"Maybe our lunch attracted a bear. Let's go have a look."

They walked back to the picnic table. Everything was just as it had been when they left. But that feeling persisted. He wondered if other trails led to this spot, or would they see another car parked near theirs?

"Why don't we head back?" he asked.

She didn't argue. They gathered their things and headed back to her Jeep. A dirt plume a ways out showed a car hurrying down the road away from the park. Someone *had* been in the woods with them. Why run away?

Annie's hand shook as she fitted the key to the tailgate. They stowed their things. Nash wanted to drive in case they needed to take some evasive maneuvers, but he didn't ask. He just got into the passenger side and pretended it was normal to be watched in the woods.

NASH SPENT a few more days at the mayor's office. He'd started in on the ledgers Caleb had mentioned when he ran out of newspapers. Those, more than the newspapers, gave a clear sense of what the town had been like.

It was dark when the mayor closed for the day. He headed back to the campground. As he neared the entrance, Annie's Jeep pulled out, heading away from town. The only thing over that way was a long, circuitous route through the valley.

Curious, Nash followed her. He stayed back a ways, then pulled into a driveway when she stopped a few miles out of town. He followed her again, this time keeping his lights off so she wouldn't notice him. Down she went, moving slowly.

What was she doing there? What was out there? Nash hadn't done any exploring in that direction. A few miles in, she turned onto a dirt road.

This valley was bigger than he thought. It was densely wooded, such a contrast to the flat prairie desert up above. She went down a long driveway. He waited a few moments, then followed, parking next to her Jeep. She'd left her headlights on. There was a house on the lot, but it looked abandoned. The white clapboard siding was dingy and loose in areas. One window was boarded up, but the others were bare. The old wooden screen door had come loose and was tangled up in some bushes in the front yard. There was a freestanding garage that looked even worse for wear than the house.

A light was moving around in the house. Annie. This place was seriously creepy. What was she doing here? He activated the flashlight on his phone, then went up the steps to the front door. He'd just stepped inside when he heard a back door bang shut.

Dammit. He rushed out the front door and paused by the corner of the house. Annie tried to run past him, but he grabbed her. She screamed, kicked, and flailed. All her self-taught defensive training vanished in her panic.

He wrapped both arms around her. "Be still, Annie. It's me. You're safe. I think. Why are you here?" He let her go.

She scrambled a few steps away before whirling around to face him. Her eyes were wild with fear, but thankfully, she was breathing normally—fast, but not panicked fast.

"You followed me."

"Yes, I did."

"Why?"

"Curious. I've noticed you go somewhere some evenings and come back in a dither."

"You had no right."

"Were you meeting someone here?"

She glared at him. Then, without saying anything more, she started for her Jeep.

"Hey. I didn't mean to chase you away. You want to be here, fine. You want to walk through this creepy farmhouse, fine. But I'm staying with you."

She stopped and turned around. He held his phone down, so only indirect light showed her expression, but it was enough to see her exasperation.

She walked back to him. "No questions."

"Why?"

"That's a question. I mean it, Nash."

He liked the way his name sounded in her voice. He sighed. "Okay." He followed her into the house. Debris was scattered about; furniture was ripped or broken or upside down. "Whose house is this?"

Annie stopped. "Leave."

"Why?"

"I told you no questions. Just—don't even talk."

"Hmm. Are we looking for something?"

She growled a mumbled word and moved on without answering him, through the kitchen, the dining room, a bathroom, and three bedrooms, all as torn up as the living room. They went out the back door.

Annie started toward the garage. The backyard was overgrown with weeds. And though the weather had cooled considerably, it hadn't been cold enough to force snakes into hibernation. He didn't care about the nonvenomous species, but this whole area was prime breeding ground for rattlers. He reached over and caught her arm. "If you're headed to the garage, let's go around front and get in from there."

She glared at him long enough to make him doubt she would follow his suggestion, but then relented. They walked to the front of the house and crossed over to the garage. It was in the same run-down condition as the rest of the property. Some old parts and tools were left scattered about. Nothing seemed extraordinary. Why had Annie come here?

He waited for her to finish her inspection, then followed her back to their cars. She stopped and turned to stare at the property, as if memorizing it. After a moment, he opened her car door. "I'll follow you back to the campground."

She paused before getting in. "How did I not see you behind me?"

"My lights were off. And I stayed back a ways. I guess you were a little preoccupied."

"You were stalking me."

"I was following you. I wanted to see what was upsetting you."

"You can't see it. No one can. No one ever could." She got in her Jeep and shut her door.

NASH CLOSED the last ledger and put it away. It had taken a while to go through the lot of them. He had a list of names he wanted to look into further, especially the top leadership echelon in place when the community was opened to the outside world. At that time, there was a traveling doctor who made stops in town. Twenty years before, the town had opened its own clinic in one of the empty buildings. In fact, they'd bought two buildings next to each other, but only developed one into a clinic. The second building had been designated for future growth.

Both were now empty, as was most of downtown. Unless that doctor he met at the diner decided to bring his practice here.

He drove back into the main area of the town and parked in the diner's side parking lot. Instead of going into the diner, he walked down the block, past the old clinic. The two brick edifices in the middle shared a wall. One had fading lettering on the front window that read *Blanco Ridge Clinic*, the town's old name. He leaned close to look through the window. Some furniture was still scattered in the front room. Looked like it had been vacated a long while ago.

He crossed the street and walked around to the alley access to the diner. It had closed an hour ago, so he figured it might be a good time to hit Betty up on her offer to let him look at the community files she stored. He knocked once, then tried the door. It was unlocked.

"Hello? Betty? It's me, Nash. You here?"

"In the office," she called out.

He stopped in the doorway. "Hi."

She nodded, focused on the paperwork spread across her desk. "What can I do for you?"

"I'm done with Mayor Sullivan's resources. Ready to move to the next collection."

She looked at him. He wondered if she regretted her offer.

"Okay. Come back tomorrow. Park in the back. After your breakfast, I'll walk you through what I have."

"Sounds good. See you in the morning."

ANNIE STAYED LATE at the diner to help Gus, Naomi—the other waitress—and Betty get some much-needed deep cleaning done, something they did once a week. She was glad they finished before it was fully dark outside. Betty was still in her office when Annie let herself out the back door. Annie should have left when the others did, but she'd wanted to finish her task. It was a short walk down the alley to the parking lot on the side of the building. The late-afternoon sun was low enough that it cast long shadows. She fished her car keys out of her purse. When she looked up, she saw *him*, the guy with the scarred hand. He was just casually there, leaning against the parking lot light, rubbing his chin with the hand she'd carved up fourteen years ago.

Annie was closer to her car than he was to her, but she was terrified he'd follow her and discover where she was living. Oh, who was she fooling? He had to already know that, given that he knew where she worked.

She'd feared this would happen. She'd come back to force their hand—she just wasn't ready for it to happen now. She'd barely begun her research here. She couldn't let them take her until she had her proof, secured it in some way so that it survived her death.

She rushed to her Jeep and locked the door behind her. As she pulled out of the parking lot, she saw the car with the others in it. The former police chief, too. All of them were here, in town, coming for her—or worse, to harvest more children.

She thought about making some extra turns on her way out to the campground, but Harmony Falls was a ghost town. If they hadn't already, they'd find her easily enough no matter what she did. Instead, she hurried right to her cabin. If she could just get there and lock herself inside, she'd be safe. For a bit. But then what?

She parked her Jeep at her cabin, grabbed her trash bag of stuff, locked her Jeep, then ran inside. She hurried past Nash who was grilling in the community area the first few cabins shared. He called to her, but she didn't respond—she couldn't.

A moment later, he knocked at her door. She'd been too busy trying to breathe to even lock it. She wasn't surprised when he popped his head in and said, "Hey, what happened?" He came around to face her, still holding his grilling tongs, which he quickly set on the counter. "Did someone hurt you?" Anger spread across his face.

Still, she gasped for air.

"Okay. Okay. Hold on." He grabbed a dish towel and ran water over it, then came back and pressed it to her face and neck. The cold shocked her locked chest into opening up a fraction, letting a little oxygen in; a little more followed that, and a little more, until finally she could draw a full breath.

And when she did, she found herself pulled into a tight hug, Nash's big body wrapped around hers in a way she might have thought would be suffocating, but it wasn't. She buried her face in his chest and held on for a long time.

After a moment, he said, "I think my steak is burning. Come with me while I turn it over."

She didn't want air between them and wasn't sure her legs would move, but he took her hand and led her out to the grill that was billowing smoke out its vents. He flipped the seared steak, hung up his tongs on the handle, then pulled her back into a hug, his big hand rubbing her back.

They stood that way, silently, for a long time. She was glad he didn't pepper her with questions. She had no answers to give him, only ghoulish memories that were eating her soul.

At least standing out there with him let her see that no one had followed into the campground. That realization let the tension finally ease from her body. She stepped back. "I'm sorry. I'm not usually this hysterical."

He crinkled up his face. "Well, two gigantic panic attacks kinda say otherwise. But who's counting? I'm perfectly fine if you want to get a few more in there."

Annie's chuckle sounded like a cough. "Don't be kind to me. We both know I'm a freak."

"Eh." Nash shrugged. "I guess we're all freaks in some way."

She swiped her hair from her cheeks and straightened her shoulders. "Sorry about your dinner."

He lifted the steak from the grill. "Well, the least you can do is share my burned food. I'll throw another potato in the microwave, and we can split my broccoli."

Annie looked back at her little cabin. She really did not want to be alone. "Okay. But don't make a fuss—I don't eat much. A piece of steak and some broccoli will be amazing. I'm just going to rinse my face."

7

Nash couldn't help the happy feeling he had as he went into his cabin. He threw another potato into the microwave while he waited for her to come over.

And waited.

His potato finished cooking, and still no Annie. He sighed, looking at his burned, and now cold, steak. He should at least go see if she was all right, maybe take a plate to her.

He fixed both potatoes the way he liked them, with loads of butter, salt, and pepper. He put hers on a plate, added the broccoli, and cut the steak in half. He turned to head out of his cabin, but she was just coming in.

He drew a sharp breath, as he always did when first seeing her. Her face was pale, her eyes like icebergs in a storm. Her bleached blond hair spilled over her shoulders. "Sorry I was so long. I took a quick shower."

Nash nodded and carried her plate to his dinette

table. "What would you like to drink? I have beer. And water."

"Water sounds good."

He put a little ice in a glass and filled it with tap water then handed it to her before bringing his own meal and beer over.

"I heard you and Betty talking about your research at the mayor's office. What are you researching?"

"I'm writing an article about the town reinventing itself."

"Oh. Where will you publish it?"

"I'm not certain. I haven't written it yet, so I haven't pitched it anywhere."

"Did you quit your job recently?"

He nodded. "I left the Navy recently, but you over-heard that too." He sent a look out the window, where he could see the great ravine. "It's pretty here, don't you think?"

She lifted her brows. "You like tumbleweeds?"

"I do, actually. And the wind that blows them around. And the endless sky. And the rugged landscape."

She stared at him a long moment. "It's different in the canyon than it is up here."

"Is it? The town's in that ravine, and it seems fine."

"I think..." She dropped her gaze to her plate. "I think it's haunted."

He smiled. Humoring her, he asked, "Haunted by what?"

"Dead children."

"Huh. Well. That's grim. I hadn't heard that urban legend yet. It kind of reminds me of what Betty said — that not all the graves had markers and not all the graves were in the cemetery."

Annie looked shocked.

"Do you want to go there with me?" Nash asked.

Annie set her fork down, then wrapped her arms around her middle. She looked queasy suddenly. "I do, and I don't."

"That's cool. I get it. It isn't good to sensationalize the dead. I don't intend to do that, but I'm curious if part of my story might be in the graveyard. Or out of it, as it were."

"Oh — you meant the cemetery?"

"Yeah."

"Could a cadaver dog find bone fragments, do you think?"

That made Nash pause. "What kind of fragments?"

"The kind left over from cremation."

"Well, that's an interesting question. I don't know the answer."

Annie sighed, as if to shake off the pall that had come over her. "Sorry. It's been a weird day. I don't mean to be so morbid."

Nash leaned back and stretched his arm across the back of the seat next to him. "No worries. It's just that time of year — more night than day."

"I guess." She stacked their plates, but he stood and took them to the sink. "You cooked. Let me clean up."

"Nah. You wait on people all day long. I get a turn to do for you."

"Right. Well, thank you for dinner."

"Sure. I'll walk you to your cabin."

"Nash, I'm just next door. I'll be fine."

He shrugged. "You never know. There could be monsters out there."

She looked stricken.

"I'm joking. Please, breathe."

She nodded. "I am."

"I was thinking of building a bonfire. Want to join me?"

"Can't. I have to get up early for work."

They stopped outside her cabin. Nash had the strangest need to be near her. There was something she wasn't telling him. What had sent her home in a panic this evening?

"Well, good night. Thank you for dinner."

"You sure you're okay?"

She rubbed her arms. Her eyes pleaded with his, but still she said nothing. Just nodded.

"Look I'm right next door if you need me. Hand me your phone." He texted himself the number of the phone Charley had given him. "Now you've got my number if you need it. Or even if you don't need it."

She nodded. She turned to go in but stopped. "Nash —do you think sociopaths are born or made?"

He stared at her. "Both."

She nodded and went inside her cabin.

Nash leaned against his dinette table and watched Annie run through her exercises a few days later. Since he first came to town, she'd done them only a few times a week, but ever since that night she rushed into the campground, she'd practiced every day, from the time she got home to full-on dark.

He'd been wanting to work out with her. It wasn't that he needed exercise—he'd already done his daily five-mile jog. It was that she seemed to be training for a fight—a hard thing to do without a sparring partner. She had her laptop opened to a video that she stopped and restarted a few times while she got the moves right.

He poured two tall glasses of iced lemon water and went outside. He held up a glass.

She nodded toward a water bottle on the steps of her cabin, next to her laptop. "I'm good."

Nash looked at the jump rope lying in a pile nearby.

Annie sighed and straightened. "Want to join me?"

He smiled. "Would you mind?"

"Depends. Can you do fifteen minutes with the jump rope?"

"I think so." He set the waters down and picked up the rope. He did the basic jump. After a few minutes, he stopped. She smiled victoriously. He grinned. When he started up again, he mixed things up with side-by-side, crisscross, and backward jumps. Fifteen minutes passed too fast. He had her full attention. Jesus, he could do this forever if she just kept looking at him.

He stopped. He was breathing comfortably. "What's next?"

"Planks."

He dropped the rope and walked over to her. "No. Let's spar."

She hesitated.

Smart woman.

"Look, you probably know how to do all of this, but I'm just learning," she said. "And worse, I'm teaching myself."

Nash smiled slowly. Some might say evilly. "I'll go easy on you. It's ninety percent muscle memory. You've got that going for you. Can I ask who you're training to fight?"

Annie stared at him. "No."

Nash shook his head. "If your opponents are armed and there's an altercation, it ain't gonna be a fistfight."

"No. But if they get me into a locked room, I need to be able to fight my way out."

Shit. "What exactly are we dealing with?"

"*We* aren't dealing with anything. This doesn't concern you. Don't involve yourself."

"I've spent my life fighting bad guys. I'm a good resource to have in your corner."

"I can't pay you."

"I don't need money."

"If you get between me and them, we'll both die."

Nash stared into her eyes, ignoring a thousand reasons why training her was a bad idea. The truth was that he wouldn't always be with her—sooner or later, he was going to go back to his team. There were things she needed to know to stay safe after he was gone.

"Okay. I'll train you. I've been watching your workouts. Krav Maga teaches to avoid altercations when you can and fight like you're gonna die when you can't."

"I know."

"It's about using your opponent's speed and strength against him rather than trying to overcome him with your superior power."

"I know. I know the theory of it all. I've read up on it. I've watched YouTubes. I've just have never had a partner to test me."

God, he didn't want to teach her—not because he thought women shouldn't learn to defend themselves, but because she was so fragile. And they had no safety gear, no floor mats, no mouth guards. He was going to hurt her to help her. It sucked.

"I saw a boxing gym in town that's still in use. I can get us some time there. It's a safer place to learn."

She shook her head. "I am not going there. Do you know where we are? The town has outdated thoughts about what women should and shouldn't do—it's a holdover from their cult days. It's bad enough that I'm new here, but I can't keep a low profile if I show up in a place like that."

There was a lot to unpack in that statement. "You're planning on staying here?" She didn't respond, and he wasn't sure what to make of that. "You're the only one who should give a fuck what you do."

"I'd rather some people not know that I'm learning self-defense."

They spent the next hour working on different maneuvers and defensive steps. Nash could tell she was getting tired—she was increasingly clumsy and distracted. She missed one of the blocks they'd practiced, letting him trip her. They both went down. Nash knelt over her, trying to disentangle himself from her legs. Her tee and sweatshirt were rucked up, exposing a wide swath of her belly and side...and the long pink scar she had.

He sucked in a sharp gasp of air. He caught her wrists in one hand and locked her legs beneath his as he stroked two fingertips parallel to her scar.

His eyes met hers. "Who did this?"

She locked her jaw and pressed her lips into a thin line as she glared at him.

He released her and stood, then offered her a hand up, which she ignored. She got up, and her shirt fell back into place. She grabbed her jump rope, then collected her water bottle and laptop. She stared at his two glasses of water, then yanked her screen door open, violently tossing them off the step.

Nash was unable to move. Her reaction to his discovery told him everything he needed to know. Her surgery hadn't been due to a health issue or a voluntary donation.

She'd been harvested.

So that was why Charley had sent him here and assigned him the duty of protecting her. That made everything fall into place. And now he wanted to know everything she knew.

He picked up his cups and went into his cabin.

HOURS LATER, he stood outside, watching the moonlight on the cliffs across the way. He heard Annie's cabin door close, then her footsteps in the gravel as she came over. He didn't acknowledge her. It was one step ahead, two back with her. Best just go slow, let her pick the pace.

She stopped a few feet from him, facing the bluffs as she looked out over the moonlit canyon. Took a long moment before he broke the silence. "What's your plan?" he asked.

She crossed her arms. "I came here looking for a place to be. I'm not looking for trouble."

"I don't think that's why you came here. Sure as hell isn't why you're training so diligently. So what's your next move? Leave before they come for you? Let them take you? Let them end you? Let them take your remaining kidney?"

Anger spun out of her like a whip uncoiling. "I never *let* them take anything from me. I never wanted any of this. I just want to be safe."

"And you thought Harmony Falls was the place for that."

"It could be."

"You got family?"

"No."

"Friends?"

"No."

"What's the outcome you're looking for with the people after you?"

"That's a weird question."

He looked at her. "Gone, dead, or locked up are your choices. Pick one."

"Killing them won't stop what they've done. There's a market for human organs—buyers, sellers, and the harvested. Much of it doesn't originate here in the States. The guys who are after me aren't the top dogs."

"I guess there's a fourth option. Revenge. We can carve them up. Pull out their harvestable organs and leave them to rot next to their cadavers."

She stared at him, shocked, as his words created a horrific image in her mind. She shook her head. "I only want justice, not revenge. There's nothing that can be done to make me whole again. But I really, really don't want you involved."

"What happened to you also happened to a friend of mine. He died suddenly after an illegal surgical proce-dure—one that removed his kidney. He'd still be alive if the harvesters hadn't gotten to him. So, you see, fuck justice—I want revenge. I'd be happy to handle yours while I'm here."

"It isn't that simple. These people have...*kid* farms. They raise children, taking what they need along the way, killing them when their parts are worth more than their remaining live-harvestable pieces."

Nash sucked in a breath. It wasn't easy to shock him, but she just had. "You have evidence of this?"

"I lived on one of their farms."

"You think that's why they're coming for you?"

"Yup. And they're already here."

"For you?"

"Maybe. Or they're here for a transaction."

Jesus. "Who are they? Point them out to me."

"They're only around when I'm alone. Usually when it's dark. They're the brokers. They show up when a transaction is about to happen. They handle the organ donor and the recipient money, and they make the delivery plans. But I think a few of them were at the diner the other day. And…I saw more, in the parking lot."

Nash shoved a hand through his hair. "Did you take this to the police? FBI?"

"Both. Neither could find enough evidence to make a case. But someone got wind of what I was saying. I picked up a stalker. I've been running since. I came back here to find the proof I need to make it stop."

"You know where these 'farms' are?"

"You followed me to one—the one I was held at. I know where a few others were at one time. They don't stay for long. If things get hot, they evacuate across the state line—Utah, New Mexico, even out to Kansas. I haven't— I didn't know what to do. I can't take them down by myself. I can't keep up with them. I don't have the resources to follow them. I can't get law enforcement or social services to help me—each time I try, the farms move somewhere before the law gets out there. I've been told to quit crying wolf."

"That's over now. You got my full attention."

"What can you do? You're just one person."

"I wasn't just in the Navy. I'm—I *was*—a SEAL. There's a whole lotta shit I can do that you can only imagine."

"I heard you tell Betty you were kicked out for fighting."

"My friend who had his kidney stolen was in the care of military doctors when it happened. I started asking too many questions. Got pushback from the higher-ups. I kept investigating despite being told to stand down, and got canned for it. But I know I'm not wrong. My friend didn't deserve to die that way. I'm still fighting for justice." He frowned as he considered her story. "How is it that you're able to track these guys without their noticing that you show up in all the same places they do?"

She hesitated to answer. For real, the girl knew things.

Nash frowned. "Trust isn't something easy to come by, but I'm asking for it anyway."

"What if you're working with them? What if they sent you to discover what I know?"

"They aren't smart enough to do that. Guys like these would rather beat it out of you than infiltrate your op."

She stared at him another long moment. "I've been putting GPS trackers on their cars. I know that's not legal, but I had to do it for my own safety. I needed to know where they were. Harmony Falls is one of their repeat stops."

"Way to bury the lead."

"I've had to switch out trackers now and then for battery updates or when they changed vehicles. They've been following me off and on for years. So I started following them. After a while, I realized they return to the same general areas. It's how I knew they'd be headed this way eventually. I came out ahead of them so that I'd be here and settled when they got here."

"Can you send me the files you have on this?"

"Yeah, but they don't prove anything. I still can't attach them to the crimes."

"It's a helluva start."

"I have something to show you." Annie led him to her cabin.

Her laptop was set up on the dinette table. They sat opposite each other as she brought something up on the screen. The table was not designed for someone of Nash's size. His long legs kept brushing her knees. Gave him all sorts of ideas, but she didn't even notice.

She turned the computer around for him. "Look."

There was a grainy satellite image of a house, some outbuildings, and chairs or something in the yard.

"What am I looking at?"

"One of the farms."

"How can you be sure?"

"It's small, remote, and loaded with wheelchairs."

Nash leaned in closer to the image, then looked at Annie over the top of the computer. "Wheelchairs?"

"After they do all the non-life-threatening organ extractions, a kidney, part of the pancreas or liver or intestines—even a lung—they take good care of their donors. Once they start harvesting them, the donors don't usually live long. But alive or dead, they are valuable commodities and are treated as such. At least, it was that way for the boys; the girls weren't so lucky."

Nash stared at her as he absorbed the implications of that. Christ. No family. No advocates. And now sex trafficked as well as harvested. It sickened him. "How recent is this image?"

"Fourteen years ago."

Nash called up a map and entered the latitude and longitude coordinates. "That's your house."

"It's all the hard proof I have so far, and it's not enough. I need more before I can go back to the authorities."

"We'll find it. So besides this image, besides the fact that you were harvested and are an eyewitness to one of the kid farms, what else do you have? Why are those guys after you?"

"I have an uncommon blood type: AB-positive. While O-negative is a universal donor type, some wealthy recipients want to match blood types. There's far fewer of us than there are of the O-negative types. I'm worth money to someone. A lot of money."

"So you think they came here for a transaction.

What does that mean? They're making a deal. Forming a plan. Lying low. What?"

"I don't know."

"Your house out there hasn't been used in a long time. It would need a lot of work if it were to house convalescing victims."

"Yeah. But it has my evidence."

"What's that?"

"Bone fragments."

8

Nash took a seat at his usual spot in the diner. It was in the back corner of the diner, which let him see most of the wide room, the front exit, and the office hallway. Annie came over and poured him a cup of coffee. "Morning," she said, once again not meeting his eyes.

"Morning."

She had the natural reticence that the town natives had in spades. It was probably why they'd accepted her the way they had.

"Need a menu?"

Having ordered from the same menu for breakfast or lunch for the last few weeks, he knew it by heart. "I'll have the Denver omelet." He wondered if she'd noticed him trailing behind her when she drove in to work that morning. If her harvesters were only around when they thought she was alone, then he needed to be near when they made an appearance.

The diner got busy after that, so he didn't have another chance to visit with Annie. There were shadows under her eyes. He doubted she'd slept much after their chat. He sure hadn't.

When he finished eating, he paid his bill, then went back toward the bathrooms. There was a back exit, which he used. Betty was waiting beside his truck with a white box. He unlocked his truck and put it inside. The older woman's face was filled with tension.

"Not a word of this to anyone," she said.

"Roger that."

Betty stared at him a moment. "I hoped they'd send someone long before now."

"They?"

"You can trust me and Mayor Sullivan. Annie's a wild card. She's in danger. She shouldn't have come back here."

So Betty did know Annie had been here before. "And Bernie?" Odd that she hadn't mentioned her own brother.

"Don't ever go into his store's basement. Or the safe that he's got down there."

Well. Fuck. What a tricky way of telling him exactly where he needed to go. "Betty, if there's something you want to share, anything that might be of use to my article, please stop with the riddles."

"Your article's a good cover. Stick with it. But limit the questions you're asking. Or at least be careful who you ask and who's around you when you do. I can't say more. I don't lie well. Just know that I wasn't kidding about curiosity ending in the cemetery. Does anyone know you're here?"

Shit. That question set off all kinds of alarms. Whose side was she on, exactly? He shook his head. "I'm on my own. So let me ask you this: what is it you want to come from my article?"

"This town isn't going to reinvent itself, Nash, not with the door to Satan wide open. Every one of us is to blame, too, because none of us stood up to stop it."

She left after that oblique statement. His head was spinning with unanswered questions.

Was it possible that this town was tied to what had happened to Kato? It was a long way from the East Coast military hospital in Virginia to this Podunk corner of Colorado. He drove out of town, heading back to his cabin—until the wrought-iron fencing and gate of the town's cemetery caught his attention. He slowed and turned into it. He drove through it as far as he could, then parked to have a better look around.

What was it that Betty had said? *Not all graves have markers—or are even in the cemetery.* As he read names and dates on the headstones, he realized that the graves in the center were the sect's founders. Their wives weren't buried nearby but were scattered among some of the outer rows.

Gravel crunched nearby as someone approached him. Of course. Outsiders probably weren't allowed to wander around such hallowed ground.

The guy smiled at Nash. A young guy. White. Dark

hair. He held out his hand. "I guess you're that reporter who's been nosing around."

"I guess I am. Nash Thompson."

"I'm Abel Crespin. Want a guide? This isn't your usual cemetery. Where you're at is where our sacred elders were laid to rest."

"I see their wives weren't buried with them."

"We have—we *had*—a hierarchy based on ecclesiastical position in the sect. The founders and leaders were never women, and they had too many wives to give preference to one over another, in life or the afterlife."

"Huh. So you're an adherent to the old ways?"

Abel laughed. "No. I'm an apostate. I was kicked out for refusing to marry when I came of age."

"But you stayed in town?"

"No. I came back when the cult was dissolved." He pointed down the street to a big white house on a hill. "I bought the mansion the prophet used to own." He grinned at Nash. "I opened a B&B in it."

Nash laughed. "Well, you'd be a great resource for my article, then. I'd love to chat about what it was like before the breakup and how it's been since."

"Sure. Sounds good. Just come on by anytime. Business isn't exactly booming yet."

"I don't want to interrupt your visit here, but if the offer of a tour stands, I'd like it."

"You bet."

The next hour was taken up with a lecture on the principles used in the architecture and arrangement of the cemetery. Everything had an intent, and all of that went to shore up the belief that life reflected the perfect structure of the afterlife. But what really caught Nash's interest was the area at the very back of the cemetery.

"What's this about?" Nash asked as they walked through a gate at the rear of the cemetery. There were dozens of rows of small white tombstones.

"This first section was for people the Society deemed unclean. They were granted a burial, but not a funeral service. They were unfit to be buried near true believers."

Nash had a hard time absorbing the life system followed by those who had lived and died here. His time in the Navy, and the work the teams had done around the world, was the exact opposite of what these people experienced. He'd lived a life of inclusion, diversity, freedom. Respect.

Until that was all yanked away. He supposed he was an apostate, too.

As they strolled past the graves of the unclean, there were rows of new, smaller marble headstones, all of them blank. "And these? They're like the others, but they don't have names. Or dates. Or genders."

Abel looked sad. "These are the resting places for the people the cult murdered."

"Fuck."

"Yeah."

"There's so many."

"That's why I left. I would have been planted here had I stayed."

Nash was shocked. There were dozens of plots.

Maybe a hundred or more. He guessed that was what Betty meant.

"Their remains aren't actually here," Abel said. "They were found in unmarked graves a ways out of town. There wasn't enough left of most of them to be properly identified or buried, so we made a rough estimate of how many were found and set markers for each of them. A forensic team from the university is working on identifying their DNA so they can notify their families. I suppose if the count goes up, we'll put more gravestones out."

Abel went quiet as he stared at the graves. After a moment, he continued. "The founders had full autonomy to do what they wanted. Rape. Murder. Abuse. They did it in the name of God. It took decades for us to say enough was enough. And even then, the government was reluctant to get involved."

Nash was speechless. He'd seen abuses like this among some of the extremist groups his unit dealt with in their various missions, but the full impact of living in those conditions hadn't hit him like it did here. "I'm glad it's over."

"I hope it is. The last of the sect's leaders are still communicating with some followers from their prison cells, sending lectures and sermons. Some of them talk about a pardon coming their way or early parole hearings." Abel gave Nash a tortured glance. "I will tell you this—if any of them do get out, I will burn the prophet's house to the ground before I'd ever let anyone in the Society take it over again."

"I would do that too." Or, more likely, give the bastard a hard exit from this realm of existence, as the crazy prophet had done with so many of his followers.

They walked back to their cars.

"If there's more you want to know," Abel said, "I can try to fill in the blanks. I was gone when the FBI broke up the cult, but I may be able to fill in some blanks. And I'd love a plug for my B&B in your article. I could really use the help getting word out that we're here and open for business."

"You bet. Thanks. I'll stop by your place soon."

Abel pointed down the road. "You can't miss it. It's the monstrosity on the right."

Nash drove back to his cabin. He set Betty's box on his kitchen table, then opened a can of beer. The box was light—he didn't think she'd given him much to look over. And she'd been so cloak and dagger about it, making him take the box under the cover of her restaurant's back alley. She was probably chuckling at the waste of his time. Whether this offered any fresh insights or not, he was going to dig into real estate ownership records next. He had a list of names involved in Kato's case that he was hoping to cross-reference with the bad guys here. But to get those records, he'd have to go to the county office. That would leave Annie alone here in town. Maybe he could do that on one of her days off so she could come with him.

He took the lid off the box and lifted out the first document, a clipping of a story that ran fourteen years ago in a local Colorado newspaper. The headline said, *Escape from a Modern-Day Lepers' Colony.*

It talked about a young teenager, named Sarah, who showed up in town with a wild story of a household of sick kids who were getting sicker every day. Asked why no one had ever heard about what was happening out there, the girl said, with some irritation, because they were sick and weren't allowed to be around other people. Asked what kind of ailment she and the others were suffering from, the girl said she didn't know, but that she and the others had all undergone surgeries to remove diseased parts.

Diseased parts.

Nash had to sit down.

The girl said in the interview that one of the kids had an eye removed. Others, including her, had bits from their "guts" removed. And for others, those preventative treatments weren't enough to save the children's lives. Many had died from their shared illness. She said she'd run away to get help, that they'd lost confidence in their caretakers.

No one knew where the girl had come from. She wasn't entirely certain herself. But the police helped her retrace her path back to the house she'd run from. Only problem was that it was empty and looked like it hadn't been occupied for a long while. No one in town seemed to be aware that anyone had been living there. When the cult owned the property, it paid property taxes on its holdings in aggregate, so there were no direct records linked to that address.

Nash read through all the different news clips and true-crime blog posts. At the bottom of the pile was a note written by Betty. She gave a detailed description of the girl—dangerously thin, pale skin with a generous sprinkling of freckles, dark red hair, and silver-blue eyes.

Stapled to the back of her note was a photo...of Annie. Fourteen-year-old Annie, eyes filled with anger, confusion, and fear.

Annie—his Annie—had been live-harvested.

Harvesters had been here, years ago. Betty and Charley had said Annie was in danger. And she'd said she was starting to see the men involved in the harvesting ring gather in town. Were they in the same network as those working on the East Coast?

Could a cadaver dog find bone fragments, do you think?

Fuck. Now he understood why Annie had asked that question. How could he protect her if he couldn't get her to open up to him?

A knock sounded on his cabin door. He put the articles back in the box, then set it off to the side.

"Nash? You there?" Annie called out.

He opened the door. "Hey."

"Hi."

"We going back to that place in the woods?" he asked.

"You'd go back with me?"

"Better that than you going alone."

She held his gaze a long moment. "No. Not today, I don't think." She gestured over to her cabin. "Betty sent leftovers home. She does that when she makes dinner for her and Bernie. Since you fed me before, I thought it only fair to share mine."

Nash smiled as he leaned against the doorjamb. "Nice. I'll bring the beer."

"I don't drink. And I have water. Come over around six, okay?"

"You got it."

She headed back to her cabin. He wanted to stop her, ask her to tell him everything.

"Hey, Annie," he called after her. She looked back at him. "You like brownies?"

"I love them."

"I'll bring them over hot."

She laughed, turning so she walked backward. "Then I guess we'll start with dessert."

Oh. Fuck. Annie laughing was a sight to behold, one that burrowed its way into his heart. She went into her cabin, but the tinkling sound of her joy hovered in the air. He grabbed his keys, locked his cabin, and jumped in his truck. Annie wanted hot, fresh brownies, so that was what he would bring her.

Bernie was walking toward the front door of his store when Nash entered. The old guy didn't look well. "I was just about to close."

"Oh, good. Got here just in time. I won't be long." Nash turned down the aisle with the baking supplies, hoping this little shop had boxed mixes. Otherwise, he'd have to try out a recipe from scratch, which likely wouldn't go well. There was a brownie mix, but a glance at the ingredients made him realize it didn't just take water. He needed eggs and oil. Oh, and a pan to bake them in. He hurried around the store, grabbing everything for the treat.

"Hmm. Got the munchies, huh?"

Anger washed through Nash. No, he did not have the munchies. Not now, and not when he'd been accused of illicit drug use back in Virginia.

Bernie cleared his throat. "My mom always added vanilla to those mixes. And she replaced the oil with butter."

Nash stared at Bernie, trying to catch up with the fact that he'd actually said something helpful. "I'll be right back." And, of course, there was no vanilla. "Couldn't find the vanilla," he said as he returned to the checkout station.

"Ah. Must be out. I have some in the basement. If you don't mind waiting, I can go grab some. I'll have to restock it anyway."

"Sure. I'm not in a hurry." But he was—these things took forever to bake.

Bernie went down a hallway. Nash looked around. He couldn't see any cameras, but that didn't mean there weren't any. If Bernie was at all like his sister, he'd probably look the other way when a customer sticky-fingered things, so preventative measures like security weren't of much value. It wasn't as if this town was bursting at the seams with jobs and wealthy residents.

A few minutes passed. How long did it take to grab a

thing of vanilla? Nash didn't really need it—it wasn't one of the ingredients listed on the box.

He followed Bernie into a hallway. He called out for the shopkeeper but received no answer. He came across a staircase. A light was on below. He started down the stairs. "Bernie? You okay?"

Betty's warning played through his mind, but he ignored it. Bernie wasn't a threat. Nash could take advantage of the opportunity to scope out the famed basement. He heard a bang and a rattle. Sounded like a door closed. Bernie cursed. Nash zeroed in on his location.

The older guy looked up, shocked to see Nash. That was quickly followed by a flush. "Oh, hell. I forgot you were up there. I was gathering things I need to restock up there."

"No worries. Did you find the vanilla?"

"Yeah, it's over here." He retrieved a small brown bottle and handed it to Nash.

"Thanks. You need a hand bringing anything else up?"

Bernie looked surprised that Nash would offer help. "Yeah. I loaded up the dolly with a few boxes. Can you maneuver it up the steps?"

"I can." He put the little bottle of vanilla in his pocket, then pulled the dolly up the stairs, moving backward. Once on the main floor, Nash wheeled his load out to the store.

Bernie came to the register and rang up the purchases. Nash took his bag and left. He got all the way back to his truck before he remembered the vial of flavoring in his pocket. He sighed. Leaving everything in his truck, he went back to the store. He expected the door to be locked, but it wasn't. Once again, Bernie was nowhere in the store. Nash heard voices coming from the back. He went that way, walking quietly, though how effective he was covering his steps was questionable —the old floors creaked.

No one seemed to notice him—there was no break in the shouting. Nash paused at the top of the stairs. Bernie was being worked over by a couple of guys who were after money. He was begging them for more time, swearing that he'd paid everything he was supposed to pay. Someone mentioned putting him in the safe. Fuck. It. All. What was going on here?

"Bernie—I forgot to pay for my vanilla," Nash called out. "Hey. You still down there?" He started down the steps.

"Hold on," Bernie answered, his voice a little breathless. "I'll be right up."

A door slammed.

Bernie came upstairs. Nash was waiting in the hallway. He checked the older man over. His thinning hair was messed up. His hands shook as he tucked his shirt in.

"Forget it, Nash."

"What's going on, Bernie?"

"Nothing. Don't mention this to Betty. I mean it."

"Maybe. Tell me what it is I'm not to mention to her."

Bernie sighed. He moved past Nash into the main store area. "Times got tough. I didn't think I could keep the store open. I tried to get legitimate loans, but the banks wouldn't talk to me. No one will do business with this town. It's dying. They know we're a bad bet. I turned to a private investment firm. It all seemed above-board, but when I couldn't keep up with my payments, they started to send those guys." Bernie sat on the edge of a stool behind the register. He looked old suddenly. "What's going to happen to the people here if I can't keep my doors open? It'll crash my sister's diner if I go down."

"Shit, man. I'm sorry. Have you let her know you need help?"

"No. And don't you mention it to her. Everything she's tried in life has been a success. Me — not so much. I have to do this without her."

"Who were those guys?"

"Forget it."

"Where did they go?"

"Oh, the buildings on this block all connect. You can go from this building through the rest, a feature left over from the old days when some of the town leadership didn't want their comings and goings noticed." Bernie straightened. "I'm sorry you heard all that. Don't worry about the vanilla. We're even."

He walked Nash to the door again, but this time he locked it.

Nash took a drive around the block and turned down the alley. There was only one car parked behind the grocery building, probably Bernie's. One building two doors down from Bernie's had a garage door, but it was closed. If there was anyone parked inside there, he couldn't see them. No lights were on that he could tell.

Which reminded him, he had brownies to bake before being late to his dinner date.

9

Nash popped the brownies in the tiny oven in his cabin. His cabin, like Annie's, had recently been refurbished. The compact space featured all the necessary aspects of a comfortable existence—a three-quarter-bath, an apartment-sized kitchen with a sink, stove, microwave, and small fridge, a dinette table with two chairs, and a queen-sized bed with two nightstands. There was a TV, but nothing played without paying the cable fee, which Nash didn't. All his free time was spent researching the world of illicit harvesters.

He opened the file box Betty had given him and read through the papers, trying to piece together what had happened to Annie out at the farm, when she came to town, and after she left with social services. Betty had included a copy of the report the police took at the time. The police had brought in the local doctor, who conducted a physical exam. Betty, a waitress at the diner back then, had insisted on being present, much to Nash's relief. He didn't like the idea of a teenager being examined by some random man in a town where she was found as a runaway. Betty was her only ally.

The doctor's findings were troubling. Annie was suffering from dehydration. She was underweight and had a long scar on her side consistent with the removal of a kidney—a fact that seemed to validate her claim that kids were being harvested at the farm. A photo of her scar cut into Nash's heart. It was still fresh, though fully healed. There was also a note that she had an uncommon blood type. Nash looked back through the papers but couldn't find the blood test that proved that claim.

He reread that report several times, like replaying a section of an audio track to hear a faint background noise. Something about the report snagged his attention. What was it?

He put the papers on the dinette, tapping the table's surface in a distracted way. There was something there. Some reason these papers were what Betty gave him. And then it hit him—it was two things, actually. One, the doctor was the town doc back then, a schmuck Betty knew and refused to leave Annie alone with. Second, there was no proof of how the doc discovered Annie's blood type. Sure, HIPAA rules were in place then, but that info should have been important documentation for the police to have in their search for her family. It was missing from the case file.

Had anyone searched for her family?

The timer on the brownies buzzed. Nash put the papers away and used a hot pad to pull the brownies out.

Somehow, he was going to have to get Annie to open up to him.

What if the doctor who examined her was part of the harvesting ring back then? Was he still in town? So far, none of the names he had from the ring back east were mentioned in his research here, probably because they were all aliases.

Annie opened her cabin door at his first knock. "Uh-oh, you're frowning. Did you change your mind about dinner?"

Nash forced a smile. "I did not." He set the brownies on her stovetop. "That pan was getting hot." He pulled the two beer cans out of his pocket and set them on the counter. Dinner was sitting next to the stove—a bowl of salad and a plate of fried chicken.

"I can heat the chicken up, if you like. I enjoy it cold, though." She set the salad and dressings on the table.

Nash opened his beer. "Cold it is." She handed him a plate. He checked out the different pieces of chicken. "What are your favorite pieces?"

"I like the drumsticks. And breasts."

He took a breast and left her one. "This is a lot of food for one person."

Annie filled her plate. "Betty knows we are both renting cabins from her nephew. I think she might be trying to get us together."

"Hmm." He sat at the table. The damned thing was

small for his long legs, so no matter where he positioned them, he couldn't help touching hers.

"So—are you single?" Annie asked.

Shit. Between that question and his legs rubbing against hers, his jeans were getting uncomfortably tight. "Yep." Now he was the one giving evasive answers.

She took a bite of her salad, then looked at him with those ice-laser eyes. "Were you ever in a committed relationship?"

Nash slowly grinned. "You're very curious."

"I am. You're a handsome, nice, smart guy. I don't get why you haven't been snatched up."

"I was married."

She looked crestfallen.

"To my job."

"Oh. As a SEAL, right?"

He nodded.

"I'm sorry you lost that job."

"I was too. At first. I haven't been a civilian in twenty years—I joined the Navy when I was eighteen. It's a whole different existence being out. The world is not like it was when I went in."

"Are you settling in as a civilian?"

He sipped his beer and shook his head. "It's not what I thought it would be like, but then, the end of my military career wasn't exactly full of the honor and glory I'd expected either."

"Right. The fighting."

"I'm still hunting criminals, only now I'm doing it without a support framework."

"What will you do if you find them?"

"Not sure. Depends how peacefully they surrender."

They'd finished eating by then. Annie put her knees up on her chair and wrapped her arms around them. The whole convo made her shrink into a tight ball. Her winter eyes locked on his. He couldn't have looked away had he wanted to.

He retrieved a piece of paper from his pocket and pushed it across the table. "I need to know—is this you?"

Her gasp was like a sonic ripple, affecting all the oxygen in the cabin. She jumped to her feet and backed away; her eyes went unfocused and her skin suddenly pale. She was shaking her head but didn't seem capable of speaking.

Nash hurried after her. He caught her shoulders, forcing her to straighten. "Breathe, Annie. Don't go to that dark place. I'm here. You aren't alone. Please. Breathe." Lifting her to her tiptoes, he bent close, meeting her halfway until their noses almost touched. "Stay with me, Annie. Look at me. Just me. Only me."

A long moment passed before her body eased, a shudder breaking through her stasis. She went soft in his hands, and then blinked and nodded at him. "I'm okay."

He let go of her but stayed near just in case.

"How did you get that clipping?" she asked. "The newspapers you were reading?"

He shook his head. "No. Your case was never mentioned in the town papers. Betty gave it to me. They were from nearby small-town news groups and some blogs."

"She knows who I am."

"I'd say so."

"Yet still she hired me."

"She's good people."

Annie leaned against him, limp. He wrapped his arms around her and spread his feet apart, ready to stand there for as long as she needed. This was a strange situation for him. He'd cultivated a fine taste for women who were sex bunnies—they were always up for a rendezvous, expecting fun and satisfaction, but nothing else.

Here he was comforting a woman who would never have a casual and passing relationship with him, yet all he wanted to do was be there for her.

He wasn't certain what the rules were, so he friend-zoned himself, cut himself off at the dick before she did. No expectations. That was best.

After a moment, her arms went around his waist. "I'm scared, Nash."

"I get that. But you aren't alone in this, Annie. Not anymore. Can you tell me what happened?"

"I don't want to talk about it. Besides, you already read that article."

"I need to hear your story from you. Those articles barely scratched the surface. I'm certain that your story and my friend's are connected somehow. I need to find the link."

"Okay. Let's clean up first. I'm going to need a lot of

brownies." She glared at him. "In fact, I may need all of them."

Nash held his hands up. "You can have all but one piece."

They cleared the table and put the leftovers away. There wasn't much to wash, since they'd eaten cold takeout, but they did the plates and silverware. Nash dried and put things away, correctly assuming her cabin was set up like his.

"Hey—how about I go make a small campfire. You're off tomorrow, so we can be up as late as we want. Put on some warm clothes. I'll grab some blankets and meet you out there." He gave a sideways glance at the brownies. "With dessert."

"You're putting a lot of trust in me, leaving the brownies here."

He lifted a brow. "I am."

He got the fire started using kindling he'd previously gathered and firewood he bought in town. The November night was crisp, but the air was calm. A few minutes passed before Annie joined him. She brought out the brownies, a couple of plates and napkins, and two mugs filled with hot cocoa. She set the tray on the arms of an unused Adirondack chair. Firelight flickered over her face as she turned to him. The air felt charged between them.

~

ANNIE PUT A BROWNIE ON A PLATE, then handed it to him, along with a mug. He waited for her to pick her seat before taking his. There were two double Adirondacks and two singles. He'd put the blankets on one of the doubles. She set her mug on the arm of the single chair near him, then went back for a brownie. She started off with the pan but laughed at his shocked face.

"Just kidding. I'll pace myself." She blew on the steam coming off her mug, then sat in the single chair. "What do you already know?"

"Fourteen years ago, a teenaged girl showed up in town, scared and hungry. No one knew her, and the story she had to tell was pretty fantastical. She claimed that she'd lived in a group home with children who were sick. She was sick too, but not as bad as the rest. She'd managed to walk all the way into town from a remote farmhouse—I'm guessing the one we went to. She didn't know what kind of disease she and the others had, but they'd had to undergo multiple surgeries. Their caretakers had been absent for a few days, so this girl went looking for them or help, and ended up in town.

"Eventually, the police chief went out to the area where she said she came from but couldn't find the house and didn't find anything that looked like a group home with children. He came back to town and ordered the girl to go with him. Betty drove out with them. The girl—you—took them right to the home, but no one was there, and it didn't look like anyone had been there in a while. That's it. That's what I read." He looked from the fire to her. "I need to know more."

"I didn't get many sweets growing up," Annie said. "We weren't allowed them." She filled her mouth with a brownie bite, then took her time chewing it. "I can't do this, Nash. I thought I could, but I can't."

Nash leaned forward and clasped his hands between his knees. "I have reason to believe that the organ-trafficking ring that held you and the others is still operating. I don't know how big they were when you were with them, but their reach may go all the way to the East Coast. And beyond. Sharing the details of what happened to you could save many lives."

Annie felt the familiar stiffening of panic, the cold wash of fear and dread. Soon her chest would tighten, keeping her from being able to breathe. She startled when Nash's big hand reached over to hold hers.

"Come, sit with me."

His voice was low, rumbly—so easy to listen to, so hard to resist. He tugged her hand and didn't let go until she was seated next to him. He spread a blanket over the both of them, then wrapped an arm around her shoulders.

"You're safe. What I'm asking for are just your memories. That time is all over. It's done. You're free. It cannot harm you now."

"Not true. They've found me plenty of times. I've had to move around, change my name—not legally, of course, just different aliases I've used. Wherever I worked, I'd fill out my employment papers with my legal name, then requested that I be addressed as my alias, whatever it was at the time."

"So Annie Bergen isn't your true name?"

She shrugged. "It is—at least, it's the one I chose when social services helped me come up with a legal identity. I hadn't used it in a couple of years, so I thought I'd be safe being me once again, whoever I am."

"They couldn't find your family?"

She shook her head. Thinking of that empty vacuum of time in her past, when kids were toddlers and kindergartners, all those early childhood years, which, even if not remembered clearly, contributed to the warm feeling of belonging...to someone, some family, something bigger than oneself.

She'd never had anyone.

Not for long, anyway.

They always died, piece by piece.

"What's your earliest memory?" Nash asked.

Annie closed her eyes. She rarely delved into her memories—there was too much shame in them. She'd gotten out, but she'd failed to get all the others out. She pulled Nash's arm from her shoulders, then wrapped her arm around his as she held it in front of her. She was hiding behind him.

"I think I was five or six. One of my friends was very sick, they said. They wanted to take her away for treatment. I didn't understand that, because just that morning, we'd been playing a game of tag with the rest of the kids. My friend cried. She didn't want to go. She was scared. I helped them take her to the car. I told her to just think how much better she'd feel after they helped her. I promised more games of tag and that I'd share one of my books."

Annie caved to the emotion ripping through her. She pressed her face against his shoulder and cried—or would have if she could get her lungs to pull a breath.

"Okay. Okay." He scooped her up and pulled her onto his lap. "Jesus. I didn't mean to wreck you. I'm sorry. Forget I asked. Forget all of it. I will figure this out. Don't go back to that place."

She wrapped her arms around his neck. She couldn't get close enough to him. She wanted to melt into him, be him, so that she didn't have to be herself.

"I let her die."

"Babe, you were, what? Six? You didn't let *shit* happen. You were as much a victim as she was."

"She never came back."

"Fuck. I'm so sorry." He sighed and rubbed her back. "But that's not on you."

"Kids came and went. Sometimes they went away for treatment and came back with stitches. I was there the longest, but then they said I was sick and took me away."

"Do you remember where you went?"

"No. They gave me something that made me sleep." She shoved the blanket aside and pulled up her shirt. "When I woke up, I had this. It hurt. It wasn't until I was older that I understood what happened to me and the others."

Nash stroked his fingers down the long, faded scar

that descended from below her ribs almost to her hip. "Did you see anything while you were away?"

"Nothing useful. A room that looked like a hospital room, but no telling where that was. They sent me to sleep when we left to go home." She shivered. "Home. As if that hell was ever anyone's home. I don't know what happened to the others after I ran for help. They cleared out of the house. The police chief said no one had lived there for years, based on public records. I don't think he ever believed me, but we had lived there —for at least three winters. The kid farms I've observed lately don't operate in the same place for that long anymore."

"And after?" Nash asked. "What happened after you came to town?"

"I stayed with Betty, but then social services took me away to a new family. I spent two years with them, then I was in six different houses over the next two years. I never graduated high school. I went to work as a waitress, and I studied for my GED, which I got."

"That's great. A huge achievement."

"I thought so too. I thought having that would make it easier to find a better job than waiting tables. Turns out no one wants a kid with a GED and no hard skills, other than carrying heavy trays of food. I'd recently decided to look into different professions that I thought were interesting to see if I needed a degree or a trade school certificate, maybe get some counseling on what my options were. I was in a college town up north. Fort Collins. I felt good about where I was headed. I felt like I had options... And then the men showed up."

Nash's blue eyes were hard as granite as he waited for her to explain. She touched his face, wanting it to look softer, not so formidable. She looked at his mouth because she couldn't take the cold fury in his eyes.

"The police were already in my apartment when I got there. I guess someone had phoned it in. My apartment had been trashed. Walls were ripped out, furniture smashed—everything everywhere had been tossed. The police took me to the station to file a report. They had no leads. They had me work with a sketch artist to make drawings of the men I thought were following me."

"Yeah? You still have those?"

Annie took out her phone and flicked back through her images to those. She gave him the phone. He thumbed through each, giving himself time to take in each face. But something shifted when he saw the last one.

She took her phone back and looked at the picture he'd reacted to. "You've seen him."

"I think so. He worked in the lab that processed my friend's blood work. You said some of the men who've been tracking you have shown up in town. Was he among them?"

"I don't think so. At least, I haven't seen him here yet. Do you think he's a scout for the traffickers, using the labs to find likely victims?"

"I think it's possible. Would you send me these pictures?"

She texted them to him. "They're closing in on me."

"Maybe. Or maybe they keep coming back to Harmony Falls because it's their hole-in-the-wall, a place to lie low between gigs. I heard some men strong-arming Bernie about a loan. The fact that they're here and you're here may just be coincidental, but my gut says it's not."

"Oh my God. They aren't just messing with me, but Bernie too?" She shook her head and got off his lap. "I have to leave, Nash. I have to go…somewhere else. I hoped I could come here, get the evidence I needed, then get out."

Nash stood. "You can still do that. Don't run. Face them down. Here."

"I think they'll kill me."

"They aren't going to kill their moneymaker. Not until they have a buyer. With your blood type, that might not be anytime soon. No, if anything, they'll just kidnap you."

Annie wrapped her arms around her middle. *Just kidnap you.* As if that was any better than being killed.

"I can drive you to and from work. Or follow you there and back. I've already been doing that in the mornings. I can keep myself busy nearby while you're at the diner. Maybe see if Betty will let me work or volunteer there after all. We can talk to her, open up about the trouble coming your way."

"She won't want the trouble there."

"I don't blame her. If she doesn't go for it, then quit."

"I can't. I need the job. I need the money."

"I'll pay you to help me figure this thing out and take these bad guys down."

Annie stared at the ground while she considered the alternatives. She could run. Perhaps she should, but this thing would always be in her life. She had a chance here, and now, to end it—with Nash's help. If they were successful, she wouldn't have to keep moving. She could pick a place and settle in. Maybe even here in Harmony Falls. The town was healing. She could too.

"Okay."

"Okay." He grinned at her, his teeth a flash of white in the shadowy night. "Now, can we please have more brownies?"

She took their plates and put more brownies on them, then sat next to him on the double chair. It felt good being near him. Really good. She looked at him and maybe stared too long, but she was enjoying the dance of firelight on his face.

"You like the brownies?" he asked.

She nodded.

"Bernie gave me a couple tricks his mom used when she made them."

"He's full of surprises." She wondered how to ask the question that had been bothering her since they first started talking. "You said you were single, but are you dating?"

He set his empty plate aside. "Nah. When I said I was married, I meant it. The Navy didn't leave me much room for anyone else."

"And now?"

Nash sighed. "I haven't given it much thought. I wanted to set things right for my friend. End something that, by the looks of it, has been long-running. Find justice. But after that, if there is an after that, I don't know."

"Can you clear your name and go back in?"

"I doubt it. Maybe I can at least get my retirement and benefits reinstated." He looked at her. "What about you?"

"If we can make it safe for me, I might stay here. I like this cabin. It's all I need right now. And at two hundred a month, it's really affordable."

He looked surprised. "Two hundred? I'm paying that a week. How'd you score a discount?"

"I don't know. Betty set it up for me. Her nephew manages this park."

"Yeah. She's totally on your side."

10

Nash's phone buzzed hours later. He'd left the ringer off, so the vibration woke him. "Nash here," he said.

"Someone's outside my cabin," Annie whispered on the other end of the phone.

"Your door's locked, yeah?"

"It is."

"Okay. Stay put."

Nash jumped out of bed and threw on a pair of jeans. He shoved his feet into his loosely tied boots, grabbed his phone for its flashlight, and stepped outside, careful to not make noise that would announce his presence to whoever was prowling around Annie's place, but the gravel and pine cones made it hard to walk quietly. He scanned the shadowy terrain, trying to find the glow of another flashlight. He went between their cabins, then down the back of hers. He could hear someone approaching. Hiding his light, he waited at the corner. A faint cone of light preceded whoever it was. As soon as he turned the corner, Nash grabbed him and slammed him against Annie's cabin.

"Whoa. Whoa. Wait," the guy said. Not just any guy —it was Caleb, the campground manager.

Nash released him and stepped back. The cold night air on his bare skin was biting. "What the hell are you doing skulking around these cabins in the middle the night?"

"Looking for someone I saw on our security camera. Jesus, you scared me to death."

"What did you see?"

The kid moved to the front of Annie's cabin and pointed toward the campground entrance. "Someone walked in and came right over here. None of our residents walk around at night, so it caught my attention when that camera went off. I thought it might have been a bear or a deer or something, but it was a person."

"What did they look like?"

"Too poor of a camera to tell. The feed was grainy. I could see they were wearing a hoodie, with the hood up."

"Got it with you?" What if he was just trying to weasel out of being the peeping Tom he claimed he was stopping?

Caleb dug his phone out of his pocket. He flicked through some screens, then handed the phone to Nash. Sure enough, the video was just as the kid described. The person on foot came right toward their cabins, then disappeared behind Annie's. Nash had checked that way. He returned Caleb's phone. The campground was surrounded by brush and some low-growing evergreens. Right at the edge of the ravine, there was a clearing that gave them their amazing view of the canyon, but off to the side, it was wooded.

Whoever had come over this way could easily disappear into the bush. He'd have to look around for footprints in the morning. "You see stuff like that often?"

"No," Caleb said. "Mostly just deer at night. Once we had a cougar. Usually, if it's not deer, it's a bear."

"Okay. Thanks for keeping an eye out. Next time, text me before you head over here."

"Sure. Sorry this woke you."

Nash watched him head back to his little house. He knocked on Annie's door. "It's just me, Annie."

She opened the door a crack.

"No one's here. Caleb and I checked things out. You're safe."

Annie stepped deeper into her cabin, opening her door for him. He took that as an invitation. He closed the door behind him, worried at the way Annie had crossed her arms over her waist and was pacing. Fearing an imminent panic attack, he caught her mid-stride and pulled her close. "You're okay."

She shook her head. "I told you I should leave."

"No. You're done running." He rubbed her back.

"I don't want to go. But you know what they will do to me."

"They'll have to go through me first."

"You aren't always with me."

"I can be. Remember, we're going to talk to Betty in the morning. I can drive you to and from work. And I can hang out in town while I wait out your shift."

"I can't put this on you. This is my problem, not yours."

"Wrong. I came here to deal with this very thing. I'll be damned if I let you get caught in the crosshairs."

She sighed and leaned her forehead against his chest. He realized then that she was fully dressed. He looked around to see if she'd left her pajamas somewhere but couldn't see any. "You heading somewhere?"

"No. Not until morning. Why?"

"You're dressed."

Annie stepped back. "Always, at night. I might have to head out in a rush. I put most of my stuff in my car before bed. That way all I have to do is grab my backpack if I have to go quickly."

"How long have you been living like this?"

"A few years. Since I first realized I was being followed."

Nash shook his head. That level of stress was what he'd seen in her his first time at the diner. "This is no way to live, Annie. It needs to end."

"I've gotten used to it—I just have to stay hyper-aware to keep ahead of them." She shrugged. "Besides, I don't know how to end it."

"I do. I've made a career out of taking out bad guys."

"If something happens to you because of me…"

"If it does, it won't be because of you. I was already on this path before we met. I am going to end them—at least this group. They hurt you, and they killed my friend." He stepped close to her, close enough to push a thick lock of her hair behind her ear.

ANNIE SET her hands on Nash's bare chest. It was cold in her cabin—she hadn't wanted to pay for the heat. His nipples were tight. "You're cold."

He nodded. "I don't want you to be alone here. That guy is still out there. I'll look for his tracks in the morning." His big hands clasped her shoulders. "You've got two options. I can sleep on your sofa, or I can sleep on my sofa while you have my bed."

She lowered her gaze to his lips, wishing he'd offered a different option, one where they spent the night together. She'd come out of the kid farm at an age where she was already far behind the social development of the other girls—not to mention the fact that her education to that point was hit and miss. She'd spent every waking hour trying to catch up. Beyond that, she'd had too much trauma to deal with to be very involved with boys. And then when she turned eighteen, she'd lost her entire foundation—she no longer had a foster family, a home, or any options other than finding work and a roommate situation. That began two years of forced relocations when the primary roommate terminated a lease or sought different roomies. She wasn't a partier, but somehow she always seemed to be paired up with vivacious, outgoing women whose personalities clashed with hers. She'd thought there was something wrong with her until she landed her first apartment on her own. It was heaven. She could set her own rules, her own schedule, her own way of eating.

But her weirdness around others had isolated her. Sure, she'd dated some, but none of those guys were on a path that seemed to go where she was headed, wherever that was. And then her stalkers started showing up.

So here she was, standing in front of a kind, powerful guy. Not a boy, but a man. He wasn't making any moves on her, probably because he found her lacking. He was worldly, and she was not.

She'd been friend-zoned, but that wasn't so terrible. She hadn't had many friends in the time she'd been free. She'd tried to open up to her roommates now and then, but her story was so terrible that once it was out in the open, they found reasons to kick her out. It was nice to have a friend now. And he looked like he could use one too.

She glanced at her bed, then at him. "We'll go to your cabin."

"Shut things down here. We'll lock up and head over."

She grabbed her coat, backpack, and laptop. He flipped the lights off, then waited while she locked her door. His cabin had the exact same layout as hers — three hundred feet of studio space. They were tiny homes. His had more of a lumberjack vibe, with plaids and tartans, but that was the only difference.

He lifted out the jackknife sofa and tucked a sheet

over it, then grabbed a quilt and pillow from the closet, all while she still stood in the middle of the room. He sat down and took off the boots he hadn't laced. Noticing her watching him, he stood and lifted the edge of the quilt. "My bed or my sofa. Your choice. You know where I'll be."

Heat filled her face. She swallowed. Crossing the room, she made her choice when she dropped her backpack next to his bed, then hung her coat on a nearby hook. She did know exactly where he was going to be. And she wanted, as she'd never wanted anything before, to be bold enough to join him there. Instead, she sat on the edge of his bed and kicked her boots off.

He shut the lights off and settled on his sofa. "Night, Annie. We'll make a plan tomorrow. Get some rest tonight. You're safe. And you're not alone in this."

She felt as if the breath she'd been holding for years finally broke free when she sighed. "Night, Nash." She climbed over his mattress and settled under the covers. His pillows had his scent. She hugged one close to her chest and buried her nose in another.

She knew this wasn't forever, knew that sooner or later, they'd part ways. He'd go back to his life in the Navy when he had this mystery solved. And she'd do...what?

Anything she wanted.

By the time he left, he would have freed her.

11

Annie woke to the unfamiliar sound and scent of breakfast being cooked. For a moment, she lay unmoving, uncertain where she was. It might be any of a dozen places she didn't want to be, but it was none of them. She was in a cabin—Nash's cabin. Still not wanting to give away that she was awake, she moved her head ever so slightly so she could peek at him in the kitchen. He wore a white tee and his jeans. She couldn't see his feet but imagined they were bare. Bacon sizzled in the pan. The coffee pot gurgled as it brewed.

Tears filled her eyes, blurring her vision. She wished sometime someone would cook for her.

"How do you like your coffee?" He glanced at her. "You know, it's odd. You've served me my coffee so often, you know I take it black, but I have no idea how you like it. Funny, isn't that?"

She sniffled and sat up. He was sharing his coffee with her. "I like mine sweet. With milk."

He poured her mug and fixed her coffee. "You've been sleeping hard. I didn't want to wake you."

"I'm sorry I put you out last night."

"You didn't. I'm glad you were safe. I think we should stick together for the next few days until I get a better feel for how widespread this evil is."

"It's wide." She accepted the mug he brought over. "Thank you." A few days' growth of beard darkened his jaw. His blue gaze held hers for a moment, assessing her. She closed her eyes and sipped the hot coffee, relieved that he moved back to the kitchen.

"It's got deep roots, that's for sure." He took the last piece of bacon out of the pan, then turned off the burner. "After we eat, I want to see if we can find the footprints of whoever was prowling around your cabin last night. Then we'll talk to Betty." He looked at her. "You think we can trust her?"

Annie nodded. "I think so. She's helped me all along, even when I didn't know it. Like when she insisted on staying with me when the chief or the doctor was around."

Nash leaned against the dinette table. "Why did you need protection from them?" He sipped his coffee, watching her over the rim.

Annie thought back to those days. She hadn't been the oldest of the kids—Emily was a whole year older, which seemed to make a big difference at the time. The chief came and took her away. She was crying. Sobbing. Annie watched like a coward, peeking through the cracked door in her room. Emily was gone for days. And when she came back, she was different. It was like her body came back, but her mind, her spirit, didn't.

That was when Annie knew she had to run for help.

"I think the chief raped one of the girls at the kid farm, though I didn't understand that at the time. I thought he'd do to me whatever it was that had been done to my friend, so I was afraid of him. After Emily came back, the men who usually stayed with us looked at me differently. They were always around me, lingering near when I was dressing, staring at me. Emily set aside two steak knives, one for each of us. She said if they ever tried to take me, I was to stab them."

"God. What happened then?"

"They came into the room where Emily and I slept. We fought back. There was a lot of blood. One of the guys tried to help his friend get Emily down. His hand was on the headboard. I stabbed my knife into it and twisted it around. I didn't know what else to do. They left to go get stitched up. While they were gone, Emily said I had to go get help, but neither of us knew where help was or what it looked like. I wanted all of us to go —in part because I was afraid to be alone and because I wanted all of us to be safe. But Emily said a group of kids that size would be caught. She packed a little food for me, three juice boxes, and pushed me out the door with the warning that I couldn't let anyone see me until I got somewhere safe. I hid in the daylight and traveled at night. It took me days to get to town."

Annie went quiet for a moment, lost in those terrible memories. "I think Betty knew I was afraid of the chief.

She didn't like him much either, because she never would let me be alone with him. When they couldn't find my parents or any family members, it was Betty who took me to social services." She stared into her mug of coffee. "So, yes. I do think we can trust her. She's part of why I came back."

"What's the other part?"

"Beyond needing to know why the harvesters keep coming back here, needing to find my proof, I wanted to come back to the beginning. This is where my life started after the kid farm."

Silence blanketed the room.

Nash shook his head. "Fuck. I wish this wasn't why we're here."

She wasn't sure how to take that, so she got up, made the bed, then sat on the corner to put her boots on.

"Ready for breakfast?" he asked.

"You cooked for me?"

"Well, yeah. It's your day off at the diner, so I figured if we were going to eat, I better take a turn."

"Oh. Thank you. Mind if I run to my cabin for a quick shower?"

"Not a problem. But after last night, it's best if I clear your space. Don't want someone waiting for you. It's not that hard to break into these places."

She nodded as she put her coat on. Outside, she went to her car and took out her bag. Nash made a quick pass around the small space, checking the bathroom, under the bed, in the closet.

"It's clear. Come back over when you're ready. We have a lot to do today."

NASH KEPT an eye on her place as he mixed up the eggs for a big frittata. What she'd said about the former police chief wasn't news — not after the notes Betty had left in her file. What had happened to him?

"Charley, what happened to the police chief? Where does he live? Where did he go after he left Harmony Falls? Why did he leave Harmony Falls?" he asked, following that question with a text of an image from one of the articles that Betty sent over. The chief's name was in the caption: Gavin Erickson.

I'll check into it and get back to you.

"While we're talking, what's known about Annie's family?"

Nothing. A few shallow searches were conducted for someone missing a little girl of her description, but no one was ever found. It didn't help that she had no memories of her life before the "kid farm," as she calls it. She couldn't even say how old she was when she was taken. Nothing surfaced in missing persons reports. After she went to social services and was put in a foster home — her first of several — nothing more was done.

Her first of several. How many had she been through?

"We need to pick that search back up."

Send me a DNA sample. I'll have a package couriered over.

"Thanks."

Annie came out of her cabin. She tossed her bag in the back of her Jeep, locked it, then came over. His door was open, so she came right in. He busied himself cooking the frittata mixture. Her hair was still wet. She wore an oversized teal hoodie and jeans that were tight at her slim thighs and flared at the hems, complete with artfully random tears in the faded blue fabric.

She dropped her backpack beside the front door, then sat at the table. "What's our plan today?"

"Breakfast. Then a walk over to the woods to look for footprints. Then a chat with Betty. Then I might like to go back over to your kid farm again. I want to walk it in the daylight."

She looked at the box sitting on the table. "What's in there?"

Nash didn't want to answer. He wished he'd put it away before she came back. "It's stuff Betty gave me — her file on you."

"Me?" Annie pulled the box next to her, then drew the different articles out. Her hands began to shake as she looked at the grainy pictures of her younger self. When she looked up at him, he felt as wrecked as she looked. In all his years as a SEAL, in all his missions, he'd never seen eyes quite as tortured as hers.

He flipped the frittata over one last time, then turned the burner off. Maybe it was good for her to see those things again; maybe not. She pulled out Betty's notes. "Why did she write these notes?" She read through them fast. "She thinks Chief Erickson didn't seem surprised about the kid farm so near to town."

She dropped the papers back into the box. "Well, it wasn't news to him. He was helping himself to some of us."

"Did you tell her what he did?"

"No. He was the authority in town. There was no one beyond him to report the problem to. And I was afraid that if I said anything, I'd get Emily in trouble. And I didn't know who would believe me."

Betty would have, he was certain. At least Annie had had her in her corner, vulnerable as she was—then and now.

He moved the box and brought their plates over, then refilled their coffees.

"Will this ever be over?" she asked.

"We're going to end this trafficking ring. But it won't stop others from popping up."

"Will the others come after me, too?"

"No." Nash didn't even hesitate to answer her. "No one gets an all-access pass to your body. Or your parts. That's over."

After breakfast, Nash showered and dressed. When he came out of the bathroom, Annie had cleaned up from breakfast and was sitting on the sofa, looking through the articles about her past.

"I can keep that box a little longer," he said. "Or I can get it back to Betty. Your call."

"I'm done with it. We can take it back today."

They put everything back, then got their jackets and headed outside. Nash locked his cabin door, then took the box to his truck.

"What is it we're looking for?" she asked as they went to her cabin.

He shook his head. "Footprints. They'll be hard to see, given that Caleb and I walked around your place yesterday."

They circled her cabin, but no clear tracks were visible. Next, they looked for tracks leading away from her cabin. Those they found. The footprints weren't as large as Nash's, so they were dealing with someone smaller than him; not that size mattered in this instance — a small person could still be a lethal foe.

"How tall was the chief?"

Annie frowned as she looked down. "I'm not sure. He seemed big to me, but I was smaller then. And whatever he was then, it's unlikely he's stayed the same. That was fourteen years ago."

"I want to know where he went after he left Harmony Falls. And why he left."

"Good questions for Betty."

They followed the tracks into the woods that wrapped around most of the campground. But once they were in the brush, they lost them. Returning to the edge of the woods, they walked around a bit, trying to see where the person had left the woods, but without any luck.

"Let's head in to town. Grab your stuff and throw it in my back seat — I'm driving."

On their way out of the campground, Annie texted someone. In answer to Nash's curious glance, she said, "I let Betty know we were on our way over. She's crazy

busy during the day and doesn't like unannounced visitors." Her phone buzzed. "She said park in the back."

"Good call. She's keeping the transfer of that box on
the down-low."

Annie frowned. "Who is it that she doesn't trust?"

"I don't know. She told me once not to risk being
caught in Bernie's basement."

"Her brother always seemed nice to me."

"Maybe the message is that things aren't what they
seem."

"And that's even more troubling. There's almost no
one left in town. Does that mean everyone is suspect?
Were they all complicit in what happened out at the kid
farm?"

"That's a great question. I trust you, and that's about
it right now. Let's just not make an enemy of Betty yet."

The drive into town didn't take long. They parked
in the back, as requested. Betty was waiting for them in
her office. She took the box from Nash and locked it
up in one of her many shoulder-high filing cabinets.
Nash wondered what else she kept behind lock
and key.

Betty tucked the keys in her pocket, then turned to
face the two of them.

Annie broke the silence. "You know who I am."

"Yes. You are impossible to forget." Betty stared at
her. "Maybe it's your eyes. I always wondered what
happened to you, how you fared."

"We have questions," Annie said.

Betty sighed, then crossed the room to close the

door. "I guess it's time I answered them. I always knew you would come back."

"How could you know that? I didn't know it myself."

"You're a smart girl. You need resolution."

"Is she safe here?" Nash asked.

"No." Betty gestured toward the couch. "Sit. We'll talk. I don't have a lot of time—we're about to start our lunch crunch."

"Did the whole town know about the kid farm?" Annie asked.

"Not the whole town. I would guess some of the top guys probably did."

"Did you?"

Betty stared at Annie. Nash was relieved that she didn't blink or look away or in some other way try to deflect that question. "Not until you came here. But when you said what had happened out there, even explaining it in the words of a kid who'd been isolated from the world for years, things clicked for me. I confronted the police chief. I mean, how could something like that be happening so near here without his knowledge?"

"And what did he say?" Nash asked.

"Not much. He sidestepped all of my questions. I brought in a police sketch artist from Pueblo and had you describe everyone you could think of who came to the house. You had the artist do a dozen portraits of the kids who were there when you left or had been there before. Except you didn't have her just do a simple face sketch. You had her draw the children's bodies."

Betty unlocked a file drawer and pulled out a folder, then handed it to them. Nash felt sick when he opened it and saw those sketches. The faces of the kids looked cheery, but their bodies were scarred. One had an eye patch.

Betty leaned forward. "I showed these to the agents when the FBI first came out and again a few years ago."

"So what happened to the case once you handed it over to the FBI?" Nash asked.

"Nothing. They never opened a case for it. They did check out the property about a year after it happened, but enough time had passed that there wasn't anything to see." She paused, lost in thought. "By then, dust covered everything. They said what I had—the sketches, Annie's story, and her medical exam—wasn't enough evidence. Someone made it go away." Betty looked sad. "Bernie and I caught a lot of grief for bringing the feds here. That's why we ended up leaving."

"And later, when the FBI came back to break up the Society?" Nash asked.

"These sketches made them pay attention. One of their team members said these different scars indicated the extraction of tissue—a kidney on some, liver tissue on others. One had had some bowel surgery."

Annie was shaking. Tears slipped down her cheek. "They told us that we were ill, that we couldn't be around others because we would make them as sick as we were. The surgeries were to make us better."

"I'm so sorry, Annie." Betty looked haunted by what had happened to the kids, tormented by her inability to help any of them. "But that second time around with the feds, it didn't go anywhere again. The investigators were so focused on their original mission that my report got lost."

"What happened to Chief Erickson? Why did he leave town?" Nash asked.

"He and I circled each other like angry dogs, trading threats for a while. Things went from bad to worse before Bernie and I left town. When we came back, we learned he worked a few more years before turning state's evidence against the Society. I don't think he even spent any time in jail, but then he dropped off everyone's radar. I hadn't heard anything about him for a long time." She pulled out another sketch. "When you were asked to describe anyone who'd interacted with the kid farm, you had the chief sketched."

Nash cursed.

"He thought he had destroyed all copies, keeping them out of the official file, but the sketch artist always kept a copy in her portfolio. She gave me this."

"Did you hand it over to the authorities?" Nash asked.

"No. I did not. At that point, they'd failed to do anything about what happened to Annie. They basically acted as if she'd concocted the whole thing. I feared this would just get swept away like everything else. I held it back so that I could use it for leverage if I ever needed it."

Annie put her hand over her mouth. Her eyes took on a distant look. Nash reached down and touched her shoulder. She looked at him, as if checking if it was okay to share her story. He nodded. "When I came to town back then, I recognized the chief from when he visited. He was the one who took Emily away."

"Which one was Emily?" Nash asked.

Annie shuffled through the pictures, then pulled one out. The girl was in a modest plain bikini top and bottom. She had the kidney surgical scar. But it was her eyes that struck Nash. They were hollow, like those of children in a war zone.

"Who's Emily?" Betty asked, taking the picture back.

"A girl Chief Erickson raped. What happened to her was why I made a break for it. Seeing my friends come back from being 'healed,' even with their terrible wounds, was nothing as terrible as seeing Emily come back without her soul." Annie drew a choked breath. "She's why I was brave enough to run through the forest at night, for days, to come here."

Betty looked at Nash. "None of these kids were ever found."

The room went silent, the horror too malevolent to absorb.

"I need to find out what happened. Not just for Annie, but for the families of those other kids," Nash said.

Betty grumbled something, then asked, "You with the government? Did the feds finally decide to look into this now, more than a decade too late?"

"I'm not with the government." He shook the

sketches. "But it's possible this is happening again. Here."

"You think you can take these guys on by yourself?"

"They're bad. Ruthless, even. But they aren't what I am."

"And what's that?"

"A former SEAL."

Betty stared at him a long moment. "Then what you should do, Nash, is take Annie and move a long, long way from here. Those who pry die. If you doubt me, just look at all the unmarked graves outside the cemetery proper."

"A lot's changed since those people tried to turn things around. They've done most of the work—the town is nothing like what it was."

"There's a reason Bernie and I stayed silent all these years. To my great shame, I chose my own life over Annie's, over everyone else's."

Nash shook his head. "No, you didn't. You fought for what was right in a system you didn't know was rigged. You did the best you could at the time. But that leads us to the reason we came to talk to you today. I want a cover for staying near Annie during the day. Can you appear to give me a job? Not for real. No pay needed. I just don't want to be far away. And there are still some things here in town I need to check out."

"Okay. But it has to look legit. I don't know who's watching. You may need to split your time between the diner and Bernie's. He needs the help more than I do."

"Good. I'll check in with him tomorrow."

When Nash opened the office door, he almost collided with Gus, who was carrying a box to the store-room. He supposed the cook had come in from the back door, but Nash hadn't heard that door close. He'd been too preoccupied with their convo to maintain situational awareness.

Gus was one of the locals Nash hadn't warmed up to.

"Where to now?" Annie asked as they left the diner.

"I want to go back to the kid farm. You up to that?"

She sighed. "Okay. But we need to bring a shovel with us. I want to get proof of the cremated remains I buried behind the house."

"BETTY—"

"Bernie! What happened to you?" Betty jumped to her feet and went over to help her twin to the sofa in her office.

He knew he looked a sight—he felt every one of the cuts and bruises on his face, and he couldn't remove his hand from his ribs because it was the only thing giving him a bit of relief.

"Let's take you over to the hospital. Geez, Bern. What happened?"

The hospital would be no help to him. Nothing would, except for Betty to send Nash away. "You have to get rid of him."

"Who?"

"Nash. He's trouble."

"He's just writing an article. How is that trouble?"

"He's a SEAL. He's investigating us."

Betty straightened and stepped back. "Did he do this to you?"

"No. I'm just saying, you've got to tell him to leave."

"Well, he's not a SEAL anymore. He's just trying to find his place in the world. This whole town is doing that. Why can't he do that here, with us?" She stared at him, then frowned. "What's really going on, Bernie? What have you gotten into?" She closed the door to her office. "Who told you he was a SEAL?"

Bernie shrugged. "It's town gossip. Everyone knows." He got to his feet. This was not good. He didn't know who Travis' informant was, but Bernie had been warned not to go running to his sister. "I gotta go."

Betty hugged him.

He leaned close and whispered, "Bad things are afoot. If you love me, you'll not ask questions."

"I do love you."

Just that. No promise to send Nash away.

"I mean it, Bet. He has to go."

"Why?"

"Because he does."

"Keep your enemies close, Bernie. If you suspect him of something, then having him near is the best thing."

Bernie knew the inescapable truth was that he wasn't long for this world. The sad thing was that he wouldn't be given a respectable grave in the cemetery. No, his enemies would leave him to die out in the wilds, where all the others were dumped. If his bones were ever found, he'd be just another nameless headstone outside the sacred boundaries of the town's graveyard.

Maybe he'd earned that.

But regardless of what might happen to him, he had to keep the evil he'd invited to town from harming his sister.

NASH GLANCED at Annie a couple of times as they started down the road that led deeper into the ravine. She was too pale, and her eyes were fixed, looking forward in an unblinking way.

"I can take you back," he offered.

"No. This is fine. I'm fine. I can do this." She looked at him. "I can do it because you're with me."

He nodded. They pulled into the dirt front yard of her hell house a short while later. Annie got out and stared at it.

Nothing seemed different from their last visit, but that had been at night, and he wanted to see it in the daylight. He grabbed the shovel they'd borrowed from Betty. They walked through the trashed house. Nothing caught his attention. It was just an old, wrecked home. He wondered yet again who owned it now if it wasn't held in the trust.

Betty or Bernie might know. Abel might be another option. They could go visit him after this—take him up on his offer to help. One thing was clear; there was still an active connection to the criminals who'd manipulated the town for decades, else Betty would not be warning them to go carefully.

Finished with their tour of the house, they went out back. The midmorning sun was low, and the sky had a hazy glow. The land felt bad. Cursed. He knelt and scraped some powdery dirt into his hand, then tilted his fist and let it spill away.

He looked back at Annie. "Where are the remains you buried?"

She started across the barren yard to a place about a hundred feet away. There was a half-dead wild rose growing beside an old tree stump. She glanced around, looking for something.

"We would bury the ash boxes here, by this rose. I made markers for each one, but those are gone. They were just posts I made from wood I took from the shed, but on each, I carved the names of my friends."

"On each...how many were there?"

"Five." She looked at the rose. "They were younger than me. Our keepers said how sick they'd been." She shook her head. "They didn't seem sick to me, not when they'd been playing up until they said it was time for a treatment. When my friends were taken away, I never knew if they'd come back alive. I tried to keep everyone's spirits up, but each time one of the kids came back in a box, it was brutal. And scary to all of us. We didn't know what disease we had, but it was obviously very bad."

Nash turned around and looked back at the house, then at the stump. "Where should I start digging?"

Annie moved a few steps over, then pointed to a spot. "Here."

The dirt was rock hard. The weather had been unusually dry that autumn. It was easier to shovel once he broke up some of the ground. After a few minutes, his shovel hit something hard. He carefully cleared the dirt away from the surface and saw it was indeed a box.

Annie knelt to look at it. Tears were running down her face.

"That one of them?"

She nodded. "That was Noreen. She was the first. The rest I put in a circle around this stump."

"Okay. I don't want to disturb this site any further. We'll get a forensic team in here." He took pictures of his dig and the box, then covered it all back up. When they started back toward his truck, Nash reached for her hand. "I am blown away at how brave you were and are."

"I wasn't brave. I was just living the life I had. At the time, I didn't know anything different."

"Do you have any memories of the time before you were with the kid farm?"

"No."

"Have you tried looking for your parents?"

"Not really. Where would I begin? I could have been taken from anywhere, Canada, even."

"Would you be willing to do a DNA test? Your bio parents may be out there, still looking for you."

"Maybe. Or maybe they're who sold me to the ring."

"Would you like to find out? I have some people who can help."

She gave him a half-smile. "You have 'people.' Why does that not surprise me?"

He waited for her answer.

"Yes. Yes, I'd like to find out what I can. But I'm not holding my breath that they are still alive, still looking for me. I won't have any expectations at all."

"Smart." He opened the passenger door for her, then put the shovel in the back and went around to get in.

"Where to now?" she asked.

"I met a guy a couple of days ago. He runs a B&B. He offered to answer any questions about the town and its past that he could. I want to go see him. You in?"

"Anything that gets me out of here." She smiled.

His heart skipped a beat.

He'd never had that experience around a woman, but with Annie, it happened over and over.

It was going to be hard to leave when this was settled.

12

They drove back into town to Abel's place. The Prophet's B&B had all kinds of wrong vibes. Once the home of the top guy in the Grummond Society, it had the structural appeal of a neomodern fortress with its windowless concrete walls around the first floor.

They drove through the estate's front gate and parked up by the house.

"This doesn't look like a place a person can just drop in on," Annie said.

"It doesn't. But the proprietor was friendly enough. Let's see how it goes. If he can answer any of our questions, then it's not wasted time."

They rang the doorbell, which sounded like an organ going off inside the huge building. Someone ran to the door and yanked it open.

"Nash."

"Hi, Abel. You said to stop by if I had other questions."

"Yeah. Of course. Come in." Abel held the door wide. "Like the doorbell? I just put it in."

"It's hideous," Nash said.

Abel laughed.

"I brought a friend. This is Annie. Annie—Abel."

They shook hands, both eyeing the other in a wary fashion. Something about this town seemed to breed insecurities.

"I know you from the diner," Abel said.

"Thought you looked familiar," Annie answered.

"I was just going to put some coffee on. Want a sandwich or something? I've got a big pot of chicken noodle soup on for tonight. Since the diner's closed for dinner, I've started to accumulate a bunch of regulars who come by a couple of times a week for supper. Usually, I just serve one meal choice, so not a big deal. But there have been enough repeat customers that I might make my dinners a real thing and come up with a menu," he said over his shoulder as he walked toward the kitchen. He gestured for them to follow him. "Of course, if I do that, then I'll have to get all the proper licenses and inspections."

Annie smiled. "Glad to see you're making a go of it here. I'm sure the administrative hoops will be worth it."

"We all have to give our best effort, don't we? I just hope this town can hold on long enough to turn itself around. Have a seat." He busied himself setting up the coffee pot, then joined them at the table. "Now, what can I do for you?"

"We had some questions about the old police chief here," Nash said.

"Hmm. I don't know much about him. I steered clear of him as much as I could. He was an enforcer for the Society. He was gone before I came back. Why?"

Annie and Nash exchanged glances. "I spent a few years on a property near here that was keeping kids to harvest their organs." She told him her story.

"Good. God." Abel looked disgusted. "I knew the Grummonds were trafficking their kids—mostly the females—but I thought that was only to other members of their group. I mean, trafficking of any sort is unacceptable, but harvesting children is a new kind of hellish behavior."

He brought the coffee over and filled their mugs.

"I'm not sure we were part of the Society here," Annie said. "But I saw the chief at our house a couple of times, and so I wanted to discover what his connection was to the Grummonds."

Abel sat next to Nash. "As far as I remember, the government investigation could only pin minor things on him. I think he flipped on the Society and escaped any charges. I haven't heard more about him. How long ago did you leave the people you were with?" he asked Annie.

"Fourteen years."

"So that was around Esrom's death and when his son took over."

"Betty said her reports and inquiries about the organ trafficking were noted but never followed up on," Nash said.

"The only thing I might suggest is to speak to Mayor Sullivan. She has most of the records for the town."

"I've done that," Nash said.

Abel stared into his cup. "Do you think the harvesting happened here in town? There's a private airstrip out east. They might have been able to fly organs out or recipients in, but they'd need medical facilities."

Annie gasped. Nash reached over to hold her hand.

"There used to be a clinic in town, but it's currently closed and has been for years," Abel said. "Not sure if there are any clues left there that might help."

"Who owns the building?" Nash asked.

"Betty and Bernie. They bought a lot of those old buildings about the same time I snagged this place. The diner had been empty for years, but Bernie's grocery store was always in operation—he just took it over."

"Were they in the Grummond Society?" Annie asked.

"Yeah. They grew up here. And left around the time of Esrom's death."

"Were they polygamists?"

"Not sure. I know Betty was married for a while, but her husband died in a car accident and her son died of a fever as a kid. That was all when I was little. I don't think Bernie ever married."

"There's an abandoned house farther down the canyon. Any idea who might have lived there?"

"As far as I know, that was owned by the Society. I'm not sure how they kept track of who had use of a property at any given time. They were known to confer property and benefits to those most loyal. Maybe there's some ledger for those things that the mayor has?"

"I'll ask her about that," Nash said.

After that, the conversation turned to more general things. Annie was having a hard time connecting this disintegrating town to the thriving national—and likely international—organ-trafficking ring that killed Nash's friend. Maybe there was something to be found here. Maybe not.

When they finished their coffee, Abel walked them to the door. As they were saying goodbye, a row of fire engines drove past the town. They couldn't see them, but the sound came through loud and clear.

Abel stepped outside to try for a better view. "We don't have a firehouse anymore, so those engines had to have come from the next town over, nearly twenty miles away. Hope everything's okay."

NASH STARED at the mesmerizing flames in the fire pit. It blinded him to the shadows beyond the fire. Maybe he'd sought that out. If something lurked there, it would have to come to the fire to get him. Unless, of course, it was a shooter. Damn, this little town was a cancer, full of secrets and vendettas and destruction.

They should have named it Disharmony Falls.

Annie's cabin door closed. She walked into the ring of light next to him, wrapped in one of the blankets from her bed. He reached up to hold her hand. She was a creature of light and shadows, strength and fragility. He'd never known a woman like her, and quite frankly, he wasn't sure he had a right to breathe the same air she did. He had so much blood on his hands and his soul, while she was made of the wind of fairy wings.

They were the profane and the profound.

"Will you sit with me?" he asked.

She nodded and settled next to him, in the exact spot he'd been pretending she already occupied. She reached for his hand again. That small touch was maddeningly insignificant. He wanted her whole body against his.

Leaning over, he kissed her forehead. "What do you make of today?"

"We have more questions than answers. I have to work tomorrow, but maybe you can ask Bernie if you could explore the empty buildings he owns. If you do it after my shift, I can come too."

"I don't want to wait. I need to jump on it first thing in the morning. It's possible, if I find that it's safe, that I can go back afterward with you."

"I don't understand how what happened to me here is connected to what happened to your friend on the East Coast."

"The world of organ trafficking is its own secret

industry—a small one where everyone knows everyone, I imagine. The doctors who destroyed my friend were on contract to the hospital. They disappeared just before the truth came out about him. This might be a hidey-hole they've used before to lie low when things get too hot. Or it could be the ones here know the ones there."

"But how did you know to come here?"

"I was sent here."

"By your 'people.'"

"Right."

"Who are they?"

"They didn't reveal their identity to me. I don't know if they are representing a private interest or a government agency."

"You trust them?"

He had to think how to answer that. "When I was kicked out of my team, I was numb. Angry. I had no plans, no future, no direction. I really don't know what I would have done had I not been recruited for this assignment. To answer your question, they haven't steered me wrong. If it's possible that I can figure out the answers to our questions, I might be able to get my life back."

"You'd go back to Virginia?"

She was looking up at him, her cheek resting against his shoulder. He couldn't stop himself from touching her soft face. "What I was before I lost everything is the only thing I know. It's the only thing I've done as an adult."

She didn't seem pleased with that answer. Shifting,

she moved over to sit on his lap and wrapped her arms around his neck. "But there are other things you could do."

He lifted his brows. "Like?"

"I dunno. Something here. Open a business."

He chuckled, mostly to cover his disappointment that she wasn't exactly hitting on him. "I don't think Harmony Falls has much use for a SEAL, even a former one."

Annie tightened her arms around his neck and rested her head on her arm. Her warm breath feathered against his neck, raising goosebumps all over him. Her breasts were pressed against his upper chest. He rubbed his hand up and down her back, wondering exactly what she was doing.

The women he usually entertained were far more worldly. All of them—and there'd been plenty—were merely fuck buddies. They'd go at it until they were tired, take a shower, eat some food, and go their separate ways. Some of them he didn't see for months. He liked it that way.

Or at least he *had* liked it.

Now, holding Annie, he felt tangled up in her expectations of him and his need for her. She was not a casual kind of female, which was the only kind he banged.

She moved her head over until her cheek pressed against his chin. Her skin was sweet smelling, and he filled his lungs with her scent. She moved slightly, pressing her cheek against his, pulling back slowly, slowly, until her soft lips brushed his jaw.

He eased his hands up her back, to her shoulders, intending to draw her arms down and put a few inches of space between them, but instead, one hand slipped up the base of her skull and grabbed a fistful of her hair. He pulled back just enough to bring them face to face. "You don't know what you're doing."

Her gaze moved down his face to catch on his lips. "Maybe I do."

"I'm not staying here."

"I didn't ask you to."

"Yes, you did."

She smiled, just slightly, in that devastating way women had, the way they indicated they knew *everything* about the world, and he knew nothing. "It was a suggestion."

He stroked a thumb over her cheek. He'd thought he was resisting because he didn't want to hurt her, but it was likely to protect himself.

He didn't know what to do with the keeping kind of girl.

"Same thing you do with your other kind of girls."

Crap. He hadn't realized he'd spoken out loud. Her invitation, eyes wide open, let him do what he'd been craving. He still had a fist of her hair, and he used that to tilt her head so that he could crush her mouth to his, giving his tongue access to taste her. He groaned and released her hair so that he could touch her everywhere he wanted, both hands loosely holding the back of her head, then moving down her back, then grinding her hip against his lap.

When the kiss ended, he was breathless. So was she. Her pale eyes were dark with hunger. Icebergs in a midnight sea. He smiled.

"What? Why are you smiling?"

"Because I love your eyes."

She touched his face with the tips of her fingers. "Take me to your cabin."

Nash stood, easing her to her feet. A quick check of the fire told him it was contained in the pit with the mesh lid in place. He took Annie's hand, and they went into his cabin. He pulled her against him as he leaned against the closed door. They tugged at each other's shirts, pulling his off, then hers. They parted briefly to ditch their shoes and jeans, leaving them both in their underwear. She stroked a hand along the length of him. He sucked in a hiss. She looked even more innocent in her white lace bra and panties.

He'd seen her most frequently in loose-fitting tops. It hadn't occurred to him how curvy she was under her clothes. Her breasts were generous mounds barely contained by her bra. Her ribs were slim, her belly flat, her hips flared. She was his dream woman. He lifted her by the waist, raising her just slightly so that he could bury his face in her neck. He couldn't place her scent, but it was light, flowery, like a field of wildflowers warmed by a morning sun. Holding her ass, he moved her body against his, up and down, letting the friction burn through them both.

Setting her on her feet again, he leaned over and kissed her, moving his hands down her hips, over her ass, feeling more than a little desperate to remove anything keeping them from being skin to skin.

He lifted her again, leaning her against the wall as he moved between her legs. Her eyes were half-lidded, her lips parted. Their contact made her breath catch. He did it again and felt her legs tighten around his hips. She cried out as she circled her arms around his neck.

Keeping the motion up, he carried her to his bed. Her next moan was almost his undoing. He leaned over the bed and set her in the middle of it. Before joining her, he grabbed a condom from his nightstand. He pushed his boxer briefs down and kicked them off, freeing himself. He was hard and ready. It was almost too much to feel the condom slip over his skin.

When he looked up, Annie was lying where he'd set her, watching everything he did. He crawled between her legs and began to tug at her panties. They only came down to her upper thighs before her spread legs blocked them. She smiled at him and lifted her legs together. He eased the white lace up her legs, luxuriating in the sight of her sex. When her panties were gone, he held her legs against his shoulders, kissing the calf of one and then the other, pressing his face against the back of her knee as he stroked her legs.

Her lips were parted, and that heavy-lidded look was back. Her hands reached for his, but he was a long way from being finished teasing and tormenting her. He stroked the dark strip of hair at the top of her sex, then slipped a finger against her intimate folds. She sucked in a sharp breath, arching her back. Lifting her hips, he pushed her higher on the bed so there was room for him between her legs.

And then his mouth was on her, his tongue tasting the sweet heat of her. Her restless hands were grabbing the bedspread, his hair, pressing him against her. Her orgasm hit before he'd even penetrated her with his fingers, which he did before the first throes of ecstasy slipped away, driving her back over the edge.

She pulled at his shoulders, trying to draw him up. He kissed her hip, her soft belly, then entered her, slowly, filling her tight channel, slipping in and out, deeper each time.

He rolled so that she was on top. She braced her hands on his belly and moved herself over him. Their eyes locked. This was the exact thing he'd wanted to do since that first time he saw her.

Sitting up, he brought her close for a kiss. Leaving the movement of their bodies to her, he reached around, unfastened her bra, pulled it free, and tossed it. And there her breasts were, heavy, with nipples tightened. He lifted one soft orb and flicked its peak with his tongue. He brought the other to his mouth, repeating that motion. Annie was holding on to his shoulders, her short nails digging just slightly into his skin, making little stinging marks that made him take possession of her hips and change the speed of their joining. Holding her up just slightly, he pounded into her.

He rolled them over again so that he was on top when her orgasm hit, triggering his at the same time. She was so hot, so slick, and her soft inner muscles milked every last ripple out of his explosive release. He groaned and buried his face in her neck. She pushed her fingers through his hair. When he lifted his head and looked at her, her eyes were closed. She kissed his cheek. One hand slipped between their bodies so she could touch his face. He thought he heard her breath catch. When she pushed against his shoulder, he got up to toss his condom.

Annie rolled to her side, tucking into a small ball. He frowned as he watched her, hesitating a moment too long. She got up and started gathering her clothes. He watched her, feeling raw standing there, nude, as she scrambled to dress. He pulled on his jeans, then went to the kitchen, leaving the bedroom area to her. He took a beer from the fridge and popped it open as he waited for whatever it was she would do next.

She paused on her way out. He was dying to hear what excuse she'd give for running out on him after what they'd just shared. She looked at her feet as she said, "Um. I'll see you at the diner tomorrow?"

Back to the no-eye-contact thing. Why? What was happening in her head? She'd held him so tightly just moments earlier, and now couldn't wait to be away from him.

"Yeah. Tomorrow. I'll drive you in."

"Okay."

She started for the door, and though he tried to stop himself, the words just slipped out. "Don't go. Stay."

She stopped in her tracks. Hope flared bright in his

heart, then dimmed to a dying ember when she said, "Night."

"Night, Annie."

~

ANNIE HELD her shoulders square and her head up as she left Nash's cabin and went to hers, but even so, tears spilled down her cheeks. She got inside her place and shut the door, then wiped them away.

She started to hum a song to herself, as she'd learned to do long ago when anxiety had cannibalized her spirit. Her breathing grew ragged, interrupting her tune. She leaned against the door and slipped to the floor, almost giving in. Funny thing about singing and crying—it was impossible to do both simultaneously. One force had to yield to the other.

She made herself sing. Didn't matter if it was a real song or nonsense words. Either served her purpose.

Nash.

God. She knew he was going to break her heart. Either when he left, or when she did. This was why her relationships, if they could be called that, were short-lived.

The thing that was after her would come for Nash. The people following her changed from time to time, which was why she'd thought he was one of them at first. She felt certain she could trust him now, which meant being with her doomed him too. She was like a contagion, spreading evil as she went along in life.

She squeezed her eyes shut, trying to erase from her mind all the things about Nash that were wonderful — he was kind and protective, brave and resourceful.

Getting to her feet, she started to sing an old hymn she learned in the church one of her foster families attended. She started out quietly and was belting it out by the time she stripped and got into the shower. The hymn ended, but she started it again, over and over. And when her breathing resembled something calmer, she washed her hair and body, then got out.

She dressed in the outfit she wanted for tomorrow, then brushed her teeth. Shutting off her lights, she spent a few minutes looking around what she could see of the campground. There weren't any odd cars parked in unexpected places. No one was walking around. Deciding it was safe, she dashed out to put her bag in her Jeep and lock it up.

This was all normal again. She was fine when she took care of herself. If she ever tried to lean on anyone, things always went sideways — or worse.

She couldn't let what happened tonight with Nash happen ever again.

13

Nash had his truck warm and running at four forty-five the next morning. Annie came out with her backpack.

"Morning," he said. His mind replayed the feel of her hair slipping over his chest, the heat of her skin…everything about their time together last night.

"Morning. Sorry to get you up so early."

"No worries from me."

That was it. That was all they said the whole way into town. Nash parked at the back door to the diner. She got out, taking her things with her.

"Have a good day, Annie. I'll be here when you get off work."

She nodded and waved, then went inside.

He took a drive around the block, looking to see if Annie's stalkers were lingering nearby. There were no cars parked in the lot or in front. The only cars parked in the back were those belonging to Naomi, Gus, and

Betty. That didn't mean Annie's stalkers weren't hidden in any of the empty buildings in that section of town. He was going to go through the ones across the street later. He'd be able to tell if someone had been hunkering down in there.

He'd been thinking about the remains they uncovered yesterday at the kid farm. He wanted to go back out there and retrieve the one box. He wasn't certain what it would prove or what evidence it would offer, but it was a direct correlation to Annie's story about that property.

The drive out to the kid farm took nearly a half-hour. It was nestled at the end of the same long, wide canyon where the town was. This whole area—in the ravine and up on the flat lands above—seemed forgotten. Maybe because just a handful of ranchers owned thousands of acres, which would explain why there were so few homes around them. When he descended into the far end of the draw, he could feel some of the tension that Annie always had. He couldn't imagine a young girl running all the way from this remote wooded area into town. Thank God she ended up at the diner where Betty was working, especially since Chief Erickson was the law in the town then.

He took the turns that led to the house, but once he approached it, he slowed to a crawl. It had burned to the ground. Nothing was left but a blackened heap of rubble and scarred wooden beams.

Nash got out of his truck. Two trucks with trailers were there, but the trailers were empty. He went around back, where he could hear small equipment running. Through clouds of dust and ash, he saw two skid steers turning over dirt, dumping loads of it on the still-smoldering debris.

He stared in disbelief at the destruction. No way could he uncover evidence of bone fragments now.

A man came over to him. "Can I help you?"

"Doesn't look like it. What happened here?"

"Burned down yesterday. We're just clearing any hot spots. Don't want this to spread beyond this area. Who are you and what's your interest here?"

"Nash Thompson. I'm writing an article about the town. This place was part of its history. I wanted to come out and see it for myself."

"Well, Mr. Thompson, you're a day late."

"Any idea who did this?"

"What makes you think it's arson?"

"We haven't had any storms in the area. And it's the only thing that burned, so…"

"I don't have any answers for you. If we do find something, we'll talk to the mayor, so you can check back with her for more info."

"Will do. Thanks." Nash left. He wished he'd kept the one box he uncovered yesterday. Now they had nothing.

He drove back to town, this time parking in front of Bernie's place. There were a few shoppers milling around the market. An older lady was working the cash register. Bernie came out of his office and waved him over.

"Just the person I wanted to see," Nash said as Bernie shut his office door. "Betty said you might have work for me."

Bernie straightened himself to his full five feet, nine inches and looked squarely up into Nash's eyes. "I don't. I got nothing for people like you."

Nash's brows went up. "People like me? What kind of people would that be?"

"The kind that goes sniffing around, putting his nose where it don't belong."

"You don't think people want a human-interest story? Are you kidding? When everyone is reinventing themselves, a story about a town doing that is spot-on."

"You're a SEAL."

Wow. News traveled fast. "*Was* a SEAL. I'm not going to leave, Bernie, not until I have what I need to write my story."

"Then what can I do to help you get what you need so you move on?"

"I need the keys to the buildings on this block."

"No."

"Betty said you had them."

"I do, but you aren't allowed to go poking around in them. They're old and falling down. There's probably asbestos and lead. I don't have insurance on them if you fall through a floor and hurt yourself."

"I'll sign a waiver."

"No."

"You asked what I needed."

"Not that. Besides, there's one floor of one of the

buildings being used. The one with the garage. They were doing construction for a while. I thought they were going to revamp the whole building, but that room is as far as they got. We can't be over there."

"What's it being used for?"

"Not sure. I think some kind of storage for medical supplies."

"So they just built that out recently?"

Bernie shook his head. "No. It was there before I bought the building. I think they were just updating it. I don't know. I haven't been in there since they rented it."

"Okay. So tell me who the men working you over the other day are."

"I can't."

Nash sighed. "Then I guess snooping is all I can do. And don't be surprised at what I turn up. I have Betty's blessing, so whatever it is, it ain't trespassing." He went to the door. "If those guys come back, call me. I can help you with them."

"The only way you can help me is to get out of town."

Nash narrowed his eyes. "Sounds like you've got a deadline coming up."

"Yes. No. It's nothing. I just want you to leave."

"I think I'll stick around and see what's up." Nash pulled up the pic he took of Dr. Mason and showed it to Bernie. "Is this guy someone you worked with on the rental of the old medical center?"

Bernie took a good look at the image, then shook his head. "No. I haven't seen that guy before."

Nash opened the door.

"Tell me, Nash. Have you been out to the cemetery? Did you see all the unmarked graves?" Bernie came close, lowering his voice. "If I help you, or have you help me, that's where I'll end up. Probably you too."

"If you're so worried about the afterlife, consider what's better in the maker's eyes—a good soul buried in unconsecrated ground, or a coward who lets himself be used by bad souls?"

When Nash left Bernie's, he drove to the airstrip just outside of town, in the opposite direction from the campground. He needed to ask the mayor whom it belonged to now. It looked well maintained, so someone was using it. There was a hangar at one end of the runway. And a windsock. No other buildings or homes were nearby.

Actually, the hell with the mayor. He didn't want to wait for the answers he needed. There was only one resource he knew he could depend on—his old friend, Greer Dawson. Granted, the guy was a former Red Team member in the Army, but they were both civilians now. Besides, didn't he have a connection to this town? Nash was trying to remember the scuttlebutt he'd heard a while back.

His friend picked up on the first ring. "Greer, here."

"Hey, bro. Nash Thompson."

"Shit. I heard you got out. How're you doing, man?"

"More like forced out, but that's a long story. Listen, I need some help."

"Name it."

"You're familiar with the town of Harmony Falls? Used to be called Blanco Ridge?"

"Yeah. The name change is just lipstick on a pig."

"Agreed. As you probably know, they're trying to come back from the ashes. Not certain they're going to make it, but I need to hit you up for some info. Who owns the airstrip just outside of town? I don't even have an address for it. I'll ask around here, but info and willingness to share it are pretty slim. I didn't want to wait for an answer. I assume it's owned, as most of the rest of the town is, by the trust the state put in place here. Someone's still using it. Or, at least, it's still being maintained."

"Hang tight. I can tell you right now."

Nash held his phone to his ear as he looked around. Where he was, up on the ridge, the view was wide open, clear for miles on all sides, high desert flatlands that met the bluest sky Nash had ever seen. Hard to imagine the hardscrabble land that the trust held was worth millions of dollars.

"Got it," Greer said. "It was privately owned at the time the state set up the trust, so it was never rolled into that. It's now owned by a company based out of San Diego. I'll do some more digging, if you like."

"If you can spare the time, I'd really appreciate it. What's the company's name?"

"Piers Industrial. You know them?"

"No."

"Whatcha got goin' on out there?" Greer asked.

"I'm hunting a ring of organ traffickers."

"In fucking Harmony Falls?"

"Looks like it. I don't know enough to say more than that, but something for sure is going on here. I don't know if this is a hole in the wall for my bad guys, or if they're working their crimes here."

"Who's got your back out there?"

"No one."

"Want help?"

Nash sighed. The hardest thing about this op was running it alone. He had no team to rely on, no intelligence to help navigate the maze. Greer's offer meant everything. "Thanks, man. I don't know that I need it, but I appreciate the offer."

"The boss has a private plane. I can make use of that runway out there. Just let me know."

"Will do."

"In the meantime, how far back do you think this shit goes?"

"At least fourteen years. I don't know if it's been a constant thing or only intermittent or if the connections I'm seeing are incidental. Right now, I have more questions than answers. Some info I've received indicates the FBI was told about what happened near here, but that got lost in the sweep of all the other charges that snagged the higher-ups here. It was old news by the time everything else went down."

"Right. I'll do more digging and see what I can come up with."

"I appreciate it, bro." The call ended, but his phone

rang as he walked back to his truck. "Got something already?" he asked without looking to see who it was.

"Nash?" Betty said, sounding stressed.

"Yeah. What's up?" He started to jog to his car.

"You gotta get over here."

"I'm on my way."

He was somewhere between five and ten minutes out. He made it in four. Nothing looked unusual from the front of the diner. A few vehicles were parked in angled spaces out front and a few more were in the parking lot off to the side of the building. He walked inside, searching for Annie first. She was standing at a table, taking an order...from the former police chief.

"Hurry up with my order now, Sarah," Gavin said in that soft voice of his.

Sarah. That was the name Annie went by when she first came to town. Nash rushed to her side, seeing that her terrible, vibrating fear had a hold of her. If he didn't interrupt her descent into panic, she'd have a full-on meltdown right there in the middle of the diner.

He put his arm around her and turned her from the table. "Hey. Can you put a fresh pot of coffee on? I'd love a cup. And nothing for him—he's not staying." He waited until she'd gone behind the counter before sliding into the booth in front of the former police chief. "You might as well leave, because you aren't getting served."

"You the top dog in town now?" Gavin smirked.

Nash held his silence long enough that the older man blinked.

"I don't care about that anyway. I'm investigating an arson case."

"You aren't currently employed by any law enforcement," Nash said.

"Didn't say I was. Where were you yesterday, oh, say, around noon?"

"None of your fucking business."

"Well, I think I'll just go have a chat with that girl of yours. I want to ask her the same question. Yesterday was her day off, if I'm not mistaken?"

"Why would Annie burn it down?"

"You saw her shaking. What happened out there, when she was a kid, scrambled her brain. Burning it would be a vindication of sorts."

"And you have a reason to frame Annie. She told me what you did out there with some of the girls, kids you should have been protecting. You more than anyone have a reason to burn that place. Where were *you* yesterday around noon?"

Gavin glared at him. "Is that what she told you? All I ever did was try to help her. Girls like her lie for the fun of it. They don't care what it does to a man's reputation."

Nash shoved the table against Gavin's chest, pinning him in place. "You got two options. Take the easy way and walk yourself out, or I can give you a hard exit as I escort you out." Nash smiled. Kind of. "Pick option two. Please."

Gavin shoved the table away and got out of the booth. He pointed at Nash. "I know one of you did it, and I'm going to prove it."

Nash moved forward, herding him to the door of the diner. "Don't come back. You aren't welcome here."

"I'll do what I need to in order to prove you're an arsonist."

Nash watched him get into his car—looked like an old patrol vehicle. Still had the handle mirrors, but it had been painted white.

Nash walked to the back of the diner to Betty's office. The door was closed. Nash knocked on it. Betty opened it a small way, then pulled the door all the way open.

"Thanks," he said, looking around her to find Annie standing in the middle of the room with her arms around her waist.

"I didn't want to leave her alone," Betty said. "Is he gone?"

"He is." Nash stepped into the room. "The old house where you were kept," he said, looking at Annie, "has been torched."

"That was the fire we saw while we were at Abel's."

"Yeah. He thinks we did it."

Annie gasped.

"I went out there earlier today. The back has been bulldozed. It's going to be hard to find any remnants of the bone fragments you mentioned were there."

"They did that on purpose." Annie looked furious.

"Of course they did," Betty said. "You two are onto something. And it has to still be an active crime ring, otherwise they wouldn't bother hiding their tracks. They wouldn't even know what to hide if they weren't connected with what happened here before. Maybe they've used that house recently."

"I have some things I want to check out. I want you to stay here until I get back." He waited for Annie to agree.

"I'm not going anywhere, but I don't think you should go alone."

"I'll be fine. It's you I'm worried about. I'll be back by the end of your shift." He paused next to Betty. "Do you have a spare set of keys to the buildings on Bernie's block?"

"He's got a set."

"Yep, but he's not cooperating."

She pressed her lips together and shook her head, then went to her desk and grabbed three key rings. She handed them to Nash. "Why isn't he helping?"

"He's afraid for you. And for him. Whoever is making trouble here, he's in it up to his neck."

"Nash, my brother is a good man." She looked worried.

"I know. But he has no idea how to deal with what he's gotten himself into."

"I'll talk to him."

"Not yet. I don't want him to know we've talked yet."

"Okay. I think all but one of the buildings is empty. They all need to be remodeled, but there's no point in our doing any work until we know how prospective renters might want to outfit the shops. One of them did have some construction started, but, come to think of it,

I haven't heard anything recently about how that's going. They took a provisional lease. Bernie may have had the locks changed."

"Got it. Bernie said the buildings should be condemned."

"Not true. They're just old and suffer from deferred maintenance."

"Okay." He looked at Annie. "Don't leave here without me."

"I won't."

"Thanks, Betty."

"We got this," Betty said. "You go."

Nash walked past the kitchen. The cook was standing near the door, adjusting some pots on an open shelf. They shared a look. The guy nodded, then went deeper into the kitchen.

Looking at the three buildings next to the grocery store, Nash decided to go into the one at the opposite end from Bernie's place. It took a bit to find the key to that lock. He walked around the main floor. It had once been a furniture store, but he could only tell that from the directional signs painted on the brick walls pointing out different departments.

Upstairs were offices. He found a door that led to an attic. There were some random things left over from the days of the store: broken furniture, spare chairs, boxes. He looked in a few of those. They had old bills and receipts from twenty years earlier.

Nothing significant there. What was important was the door that led through to the next building. It wasn't locked. Bernie had said the buildings were all connected. The choice now was whether to go to the next building or first tour the basement of this one.

Deciding he could always come back and do the basement later, he went through to the door. That attic also had a thick layer of dust covering odd leftover pieces of furniture. He wondered if that space had been a spillover for the furniture store back in the day. Maybe the rest of the building was also part of the old showroom. Didn't look like anyone had been through there lately.

The stairs led down to the second floor. It had been divided into separate offices, with locks. They were tiny and uninteresting. The main floor also had offices. Looked like it might have once been a doctor's office. The basement had alley access through a big garage door. Between the garage area and front half of that floor was a steel room with a ramp to a wide door. None of the keys Betty gave him worked on it. He knocked on the door to see if anyone was there, but unsurprisingly, no one answered. He looked up to the camera that was pointed toward the door.

A wall of reinforced steel and a security camera.

Maybe that made sense for a medical storage locker. Maybe not.

Nash returned to the attic and moved on to the third building. This one was empty from top to bottom, other than a thick coating of dust everywhere. Like the others, this one had a door that went into the attic of the grocery store. That door was unlocked. He left that for now and went to check out the other floors of the building.

The main floor looked as if it had at one time—in better days—been an extension of the grocery store. Maybe it would be that again, when the town was revived. The doors between the two areas of the main level were locked. He went down to the basement. It was empty, except for the artifacts of its prior use—old crates, empty boxes, dusty shelves holding broken things. Here, too, was a double door between the two buildings. This one was not locked, which was probably no more of a security breach than the shared attic access that spanned the block.

Nash walked through the doors into Bernie's storage room. The guys beating him up probably came through one of the other buildings to avoid detection. What Nash needed to set up were cameras. About a dozen of them. And some for the cabins where he and Annie were staying. Even though Charley said she had eyes on their places, he wanted a more direct feed. Maybe at the diner too.

His phone vibrated; he'd put it on silent mode when he began his tour of the buildings, just in case he ran into anyone. He went back through to the next building, then answered.

"Yo. Nash."

"Hey, Greer."

"I did some more digging. The company that owns the airstrip is a shell company that bounces through four others, ending up in the UAE."

"Fuck." That was not good news. It corroborated Charley's suspicions. Whoever was running this branch of the organ network, they had made a sizable investment in their infrastructure in Harmony Falls, between the airfield and the medical storage facility. None of that was something anyone would do for a one-off transaction.

"Yeah. I can keep poking around. But something else I found curious is that one of the buildings in that block with the grocery store has an active account with the rural power company. Water too. No other utilities. The accounts are paid on time."

"Who holds the account?"

"Bernie Carson."

"No kidding."

"Yeah, I'm not kidding. I have better jokes than that."

"I knew Bernie was renting out one of the buildings, but I hoped the renters had taken accounts in their own names rather than running them through him. Thanks. I'll push more from this side. I have to run up to Grand Junction to pick up some security cameras. I need to see who's coming and going from this place."

"Bro, security is my deal. Shit, why didn't you tell me you needed that? I can bring some down tomorrow. How many do you need?"

"Twelve. All around and inside this block of buildings, and two out at the cabins my friend and I are renting."

"Friend, huh?"

"Friend."

"Hmm. Well, with that many, I think I'll swing by and pick up Levi Jones. The three of us can knock it out pretty quickly. Or four if your friend's helping."

"She's not. Really, I want to stay quiet about this, so let's do it at night. And since when is Levi in town?"

"You didn't know? He settled in NoCo when he left the teams. He's farming sunflowers or some shit and also doing security work. He too found a *friend*. He's married to her now. But he owes my guys a favor, so I'll call it in. We can talk more when we get there."

"Thanks, man. I owe you."

"I know. And one day I'll call it in. See you tomorrow."

14

Nash waited in the dark alley behind the row of brick shops. He'd taken Annie out to Abel's after her shift. And he also reserved rooms for Greer and Levi. A black SUV pulled into the alley and parked facing Nash's truck. His two friends got out, dressed all in black, with ski masks rolled up to their foreheads.

Nash laughed as he greeted them. "Did you wear those damned things the whole way down?"

"You shoulda seen the looks going through Denver." Levi laughed. They exchanged a bro hug.

"Heard you were out, but didn't know you'd settled in Colorado," Nash said.

"Yeah. It all worked out for me. And what the fuck happened to you? You're the last person I'd have expected to be run out of the teams."

"Me too. I guess that's what happens when you don't let sleeping dogs lie. Let's get these cameras up, then we can talk later. I'd love your input."

Nash gave the guys a walk-through of the areas where he wanted cameras. They settled on having them on either side of Bernie's basement access, either side of his attic access, four in the alley itself, positioned across from the entrances, facing each of the buildings, and two out front. That left him two to put up at the cabins, which he could do later.

"Let's stay clear of the second building over," Nash said. "Someone has done some remodeling in there. I noticed a camera in the garage area."

"If it's actively monitored, then they know you've been poking around." Greer looked over that way. "It's the only building with a garage."

"Right on both accounts. And besides the grocery store, it's the only one that's in use or has recently been in use," Nash said. "Let's get this done. If they come looking for me, I want to know who they are."

When they finished, Greer downloaded the operating software to Nash's phone while Levi stowed their tools. "You gotta know, these are Owen's cameras," Greer said, "so they're feeding into our systems. We're not going to be monitoring them, unless you call us. But we'll have the feeds if you need to retrieve them."

"Owen?" Nash asked.

"Tremaine."

"Shit. You're working for him?"

"Yeah. And keep it in mind. He's always looking to grow his team."

That was an option Nash hadn't expected. "Does he know I was kicked out?"

"He will when I tell him. He takes our recs seriously, though, so you've got a job if you want it."

"Okay. Thanks. Let's head over to your rooms at the Prophet's B&B."

"The what now?" Levi asked.

"This whole town used to be privately owned by an isolationist religious cult called the Grummond Society that practiced polygamy," Nash said. "It's now in a state-held trust meant to assist the Society's victims. The leaders called themselves prophets, demanding allegiance and loyalty from their followers. A former member bought the last prophet's residence and opened a B&B."

"I hate that place," Greer said.

Nash laughed. "Agreed. It should be a year-round Halloween horror house. But the proprietor, Abel, is a good guy."

"You trust him?" Levi asked.

"Yeah," Greer said. "I've checked him out a couple of times." At Levi and Nash's surprised reaction, he explained. "My wife spent most of her childhood in the cult. We've come here a few times, and I always like to know who I'm dealing with."

"Good to know," Nash said.

"Let's get out of here," Greer said. "I want to hear how you ended up in this random place."

"I don't think it is random, but I can't see the connections yet."

At the B&B, the lights were still on. The door was locked, so they rang the doorbell. Abel opened it, looking cheery. Nash glanced at Levi and Greer, wondering how Abel would react to their being dressed in tactical gear, but he didn't seem fazed.

"All done with your secret mission?" Abel asked.

"Yep," Nash answered. "Annie good?"

"She's fine. Good to see you again." Abel shook hands with Greer.

"Same," Greer said. "This is our friend Levi."

"Nice to meet you, Levi. We made you all some dinner. Didn't know if you'd eaten."

"I'm starved," Levi said. "Greer doesn't believe in stopping for anything other than gas."

Abel led the way to the kitchen. Annie got up from the table. She looked at each of them, then lowered her gaze and clenched her hands. Nash went over and pulled her close. "These are my friends, Annie. You can trust them. Levi was in the Navy until recently. And even though Greer was Army, we still like him."

Annie nodded but pulled away from Nash and went to help Abel serve the dinner they'd made — lasagna, salad, and garlic bread. Abel brought over a pitcher of iced tea.

Levi looked at it, then asked, "You got any beer, Abel?"

"Nope. No alcohol in this house." Abel sighed. "I should probably get over that. I still find the Grummonds have rewired my life in so many unexpected ways. But anyway. I have water if you don't want tea."

Levi chuckled. "Tea works. Thanks."

They washed up, then filled their plates and settled around the table.

"Anyone else here, Abel?" Nash asked.

"No. You guys are my only visitors, and it's just me in the house tonight. Knowing you were coming, I didn't open for dinner."

"Thanks," Greer said. "So spill, Nash. What's going on?"

Nash felt Annie's tension ratchet up. He decided to avoid telling her portion of the story. "I don't know if you know why I was forced out of the teams."

"I heard rumors," Levi said, "but I don't believe them."

"It's not why you think or what you've heard. My friend, Kato, was injured in one of our recent ops. A bullet shattered his shoulder blade and ripped his lung apart, just missing his heart. It was bad, but his prognosis was good. He was taken to the VA hospital, but transferred to a civilian hospital specializing in thoracic injuries. Somewhere between the two hospitals, he was briefly diverted and had a kidney illegally harvested. My investigation into what the fuck happened started to push up against some powerful people. When I tried to find out how involved they were and how pervasive 'mistakes' like what happened to Kato were, I ran into trouble with my command. I was told to stop, but I didn't. They screwed with a pee test I took, then came up with faked evidence that I'd been dealing on base, hence my other-than-honorable discharge."

"Was Kato an organ donor?" Levi asked.

"Yes. But his kidney incision had begun healing by the time he died two weeks later. The hospitals involved were forced to admit to the 'error,'" Nash said, making air quotes. "However, no one could account for whatever happened to his kidney."

"So what brought you here?" Greer asked.

"I'm still trying to figure that out." Nash looked at his friends, knowing this part of the story was hard to digest. "The day I walked off the base, I got a call from a woman representing a mysterious group. She left a map in my truck, a phone, some cash, and told me my answers were out here, in this...town."

Greer and Levi swapped glances. "Was that the same one who recruited you?" Greer asked Levi.

"I don't know if they're connected, but my handler was Commander Lambert."

"Mine is a woman named Charley. I know nothing about who she is, who she represents. She offered an obscene amount of money to come here and solve the mystery. I came because I'd run out of leads back in Virginia—not for the money, which I haven't accepted."

"And what have you found?" Greer asked.

"Only that there was a house a few miles from here that once held children who were being live-harvested for parts."

Annie went stiff beside him.

Levi looked disgusted. "When was that happening?"

"Fourteen years ago," Nash answered. "So we know

an organ-trafficking ring did exist here once." He looked at Abel. "It was that house that burned the other day."

"That can't be a coincidence. Who did it?" Abel asked.

"I don't know yet. But the town's former police chief came sniffing around the diner, asking questions, acting as if he was hired to investigate it."

"Text me his name," Greer said. "I'll look into him. What else you got? You said the diner? That place was lousy with ghosts."

"Some people say the same about this place," Abel said.

"They're right." Greer chuckled.

"Wait, you see ghosts?" Levi asked.

"Yeah. He does," Nash said.

"Most of the ones around town aren't malicious," Greer said. "They just want to be heard. They want vindication for what happened to them in life. But anyway, so someone bought the diner?"

"Yep," Nash said. "A brother and sister team. They were part of the old cult but got out and recently came back. Besides the diner, they bought the row of buildings across the way, including the grocery store business itself. Two of the buildings in his block have remained unused. And Bernie said one was undergoing some renovations, but those have been paused for some reason. He said he wasn't sure what business was going in there. Thought it was some kind of medical storage or something. He'd agreed to let them do some renovation, but it seems it only got so far and then stopped. I've been through the whole row of buildings. That room is the only interesting spot in all of them, but it's got tight security. Without blowing it open, I couldn't get in there."

Greer shook his head. "You need to get you some skills, son."

Nash chuckled. Greer was a good eight years younger than him, but he'd been in private security longer.

Levi laughed. "It's good we're here."

"The house where the kids were stowed and the old police chief are the only connections I've found that I can link with the organ trafficking that was here before," Nash said. "Not much to go on."

"What's the chief's involvement?" Levi asked.

"He moved kids around for the keepers," Nash said.

"I was there." Annie had been listening intently. All eyes went to her as she stood and showed her old surgery scar. "He did worse than that. He abused the girls being held there. I ran away before he could get to me."

"Fuck," Greer said. "So his poking around now is curious timing."

"Not if he's the arsonist who burned Annie's kid farm down," Abel said. "I always hated that man."

"The other thing, and I have no idea if it's connected, is that Bernie's gotten himself tangled up with some loan sharks," Nash said. "They keep working him over. He's trying to keep it from his sister, but I don't know how long he can do that. I'm hoping he'll let me help, but he's digging his heels in."

"Yep. Give me those names too," Greer said.

"He won't tell me. But they get in to his store, and now I know how, so we'll hopefully get some faces we can work with."

Greer pushed his plate away, then leaned back. "Look, I can be here as long as you need me. This is my wife's hometown. And though she has a love/hate relationship with it, I feel as if we have a stake in its survival." He looked at Levi. "If you can't stay, no worries. Take my car back. I'll get it when I return. Or one of my team can come to your place to pick it up."

"I'm good. I want to see this through."

Abel got up. "I just thought of something. Hold on." He left the room and came back a moment later with a canvas ledger. "Everyone signs in when they come here. Mandatory. There aren't a lot of places to stay around here. If Bernie's renters took rooms, we'd have their names. I can confirm that the names in here match their IDs and billing info. Of course, they might have just camped in any of the empty buildings or houses over there."

"Do you have a Dr. Mason in your log?" Annie asked quietly.

"Who's that?" Levi looked at her.

"He's a doctor who comes to town now and then," she said.

Nash handed the doctor's card to Greer. "He mentioned he might be thinking of opening a practice in a town like this one that needs a doctor and a clinic."

"Yes. I do have him in here," Abel said. "He was here just a few days ago."

"I asked Bernie if he recognized him, but he didn't," Nash said. "Maybe he's who leased that space. I need to get Bernie to open up to me."

"I can talk to him," Annie offered. "You guys are a little—a lot—overwhelming. It might be less bruising to his ego if he spoke to me about all of it than if you try to drag it out of him."

Silence hit the room.

Nash slowly smiled. "I like it. Let's do that. I'll be nearby the whole time."

"But out of sight," she insisted.

"Right."

"We'll all be nearby," Greer said. "I can rig you up with two-way tech so we can help guide your convo, if needed."

"So what's your next step?" Abel asked.

"Greer's got some research to do," Nash said. "I think you and Levi should stay out of sight for a while. Newcomers arouse suspicion."

"Or maybe stirring things up will help get things moving along," Levi said, grinning. "Besides, you've already been spotted snooping around, so it's not like we have a choice."

"You always did prefer the wrecking-ball approach," Nash said with a chuckle.

"Works. Most times."

"Fine." Nash shook his head. "Balls to the wall it is."

Levi started clearing the table. "Can we help wash up?"

"No," Abel said. "I got this. Go plan your war games. I'll see what else I can find in my log."

Annie was putting food away when Nash came up to her. He put an arm around her and kissed her forehead. "You were brave to volunteer," he said quietly.

"I want to help. I *need* to help."

Nash nodded. "I'm just going to give the guys a hand getting their stuff. I'll be right back."

Greer and Levi followed him out to their SUV. Nash texted Greer the name of Betty's main cook. "Look into this guy too. I didn't say anything in front of Annie because I don't want to freak her out. She's got to work with him, and I don't want his focus on her if she starts acting weird around him. I don't know if he's involved in any way, but there's something about him. He always seems to be lingering nearby when I'm talking to Betty."

"Let's feed him some intel," Levi suggested. "We can see what shifts after that."

Nash agreed. "Good. We'll do that tomorrow."

"I'll get his background and send you an update," Greer said. "I wish we had the names of Bernie's extortionists, but stirring things up with the cook might get things rolling."

∽

NASH, Annie, Greer, and Levi were sitting in Greer's room a few hours later. Nash started to pace. "What if it's just some loan sharks Bernie got himself tangled up with that we're working with? Maybe they're here not to harvest organs but to capitalize on the growth the town's after in reinventing itself. Maybe my contact got it all wrong, based solely on the town's old history."

"Handlers like yours don't usually make rookie mistakes," Levi said.

"The loan sharks could be a distraction," Greer said. "What do they get by playing this game?"

"Depends if they're just here because this is a weak town and there's a buck to be made," Nash said, "but that's a lot of effort for little return. Maybe the Society left a stash of riches behind that they want to find. Their thuggery could cover their search."

"But if your handler is right, and what's here overlaps what you were working on back east, then their work distracting you would let them do what?" Annie asked.

"We haven't seen inside that new medical storage unit yet," Greer said.

Nash shoved his hands in his hair. "What if they've lined up a procedure? What if they're bringing in donor and recipient?"

"What if their donor is already here?" Annie asked.

Nash turned and stared at her. She'd voiced his greatest fear.

"You let him prowl through our building," Travis said.

Bernie drew a shaky breath. It was unnerving getting a phone call from the guy heading up the loan-sharking business he'd inadvertently used.

"No. I didn't," Bernie replied. "I specifically told him all the buildings were off-limits to him."

"We have video of him."

"What are you doing over there that's so secret, anyway? I thought you were building out a medical storage facility."

"What we're doing is none of your business."

"Well, actually, it is. I own the building."

Travis chuckled. "Not for long. You're going to be signing it over to us very soon."

"No. I won't. I'll go to the media and tell them everything. You want secrecy, but you won't have it if you keep threatening me. I paid you back according to our original terms. I don't owe you another dime."

"You paid late. Our terms stipulated what would happen in that situation."

Bernie hung up. He opened a search screen and stared at it, trying to figure out the best way to find a reputable news outlet that covered crime in small towns. A quick search showed him it wasn't going to be an easy thing to find. These thugs weren't even from this state, if he were to judge from their mid-East Coast accents.

His phone rang. He stared at it. If he didn't answer, he wouldn't have to hear their threats. It stopped ringing. A text popped up.

Pick up your phone.

It rang again. It stopped, then rang again.

Bernie set his phone to record, then answered. "What?"

"What? Quite the little big man, aren't you?" Travis again. "People like you want to believe you have power over your own life. But you don't. You only have the power granted to you from everyone better than you. But I will gift you a moment of autonomy. You may make a choice about who dies next. Nash or your beloved sister."

"Why should anyone die? I've repaid my loan to you. We're done doing business. And since the people you work for have not paid their rent in the last three months, you can tell them they're done, too. I'm changing the locks in the morning."

"Your sister it is." The call ended, then a text came

in. *Kill Nash, and I will spare your sister.*

Bernie called his sister. "I need to talk to you."

"Sure," Betty said. "You don't have to call, just come over. What's going on, Bernie?"

"I'll tell you when we talk."

ANNIE SAW BERNIE hang up the phone as she stepped into his office. When he wasn't out in the store, she always knew where she could find him. Betty had sent her over with a list plenty of times. She supposed neither of them texted.

Betty's brother did not look well. He was pale and sweating.

"Bernie? Everything okay?" Annie asked.

It took him a moment to respond, almost as if he wasn't aware she was in the room. "Yes." He looked up at her from his desk. "Yeah, everything's fine."

She shook her head. "Everything is not fine. I know 'not fine.' I've lived with 'not fine' my entire life. I've pretended it was. I've hoped it would be. I've hated myself for what I was and wasn't. I'm a master of not fine. And fake fine is even worse. Tell me what's going on, because living how you are is not living."

Bernie dropped his head into his hands. His answer was a little muffled. "They're going to kill me."

"Who is?"

He straightened and stared at her as if wrestling demons she couldn't see. "I borrowed money from people I shouldn't have. They required an exorbitant interest rate. I paid it all back, but I was late, so they doubled the amount I owe, and now they are threatening to seize this building."

Annie perched on the edge of his desk. "Have you talked to your sister?"

"No. I can't. Neither of us has the kind of money they are demanding. And if I speak to anyone, well, something awful will happen."

"Nash can help."

"He's just one guy."

"He has friends in town."

Bernie mopped his head with a handkerchief. "It's bad enough that I'm in this situation, but to drag anyone else into it just won't do."

"Bernie, your sister depends on you. What would she do if something happened to you?"

She had his attention. He hadn't thought of things from that perspective.

"Nash was a SEAL. He doesn't talk about it much, but he's spent his whole career dealing with bad guys. He knows how to help. So do his friends. I believe in them, and I believe in you. Let's go over and talk to Betty."

BERNIE LOCKED up the store behind him and Annie. Nash was there to meet them. "What are you doing here?" Bernie asked him.

"I came for Annie," Nash said.

"Take her. And go home."

"I don't think so, Bernie."

"I mean it, Nash. You should never have gone snooping around my buildings."

"Uh-huh. Well, I did. What's done is done. Let's go talk to Betty. She should be told what you've gotten yourself into." Nash paused. "She deserves to know, doesn't she, since her life is on the line."

Annie gasped. "Bernie!" She stared at him in shock, then shook her head.

Nash took her elbow. "We can't talk here. Let's get inside the diner."

Bernie let out an exasperated sigh and started across the street with them.

The diner was locked, as it was nearing four o'clock, but Betty was there to let them in. She gave them each a questioning glance, then locked the front door and led the way to her office.

Gus was in the storeroom. Hearing them come down the hallway, he came to the doorway of the supply room. As Nash was the last in line, he caught the meaningful glance the cook gave Bernie. Interesting. And as expected. Nash closed the door to Betty's office. He wanted Bernie to be comfortable enough to speak freely. Nash stood at the door, ready to yank it open to see if he could catch the cook eavesdropping. If so, well, Nash would start counting bodies.

Bernie paced the room. Betty took hold of Annie's hand and drew her over to the sofa. For a moment,

Betty just watched Bernie. "Wearing a hole in my floor isn't going to help," she said.

He stopped, then turned and looked at her. "I've done something very bad."

"Okay."

"I took a loan. A non-traditional loan."

"From those men I've been seeing around your place."

Bernie nodded. "I don't really know who they are." He looked at Nash. And damn, if looks could kill, Nash thought. "They seemed so accommodating, so willing to assist a merchant trying to help his town. But I couldn't fully repay them in the short window they gave me."

"Bern, why didn't you say something?"

Bernie looked infuriated. "Because you are always successful. Everything you do works. You've never had a hard time making ends meet."

"That's not true at all. You know life was a struggle for a long time after we left the Society."

"Well, I couldn't tell you. I didn't want to worry you. I didn't want you to think I couldn't get myself out of what I got myself into. I did pay their loan back, with interest, but since I paid it back late, they doubled the amount I owed. I can't pay that. You can't pay that. They're threatening our lives, Bet."

"Oh."

"Who are they, Bernie?" Nash asked.

Bernie's face wrinkled into a snarl. He came over to poke his finger into Nash's chest. "You're what set them off. I'm sure they would have forgiven my slow repayment if it weren't for you. They know you're a SEAL. They want me to kill you."

"*Was* a SEAL. How do they know that? And what difference does my being here in town make—unless they were planning on sticking around and extorting other people?"

Bernie glared at him. He almost said something, but then clamped his mouth shut. Nash reached over and yanked the office door open, just in time to catch a shadow of movement. Maybe that was just the cook going into the kitchen from the supply room. Maybe Nash had been a second late trying to catch him.

He supposed he had his answer about how the loan sharks knew a former SEAL was in town. Nash followed Gus into the kitchen. He found him crouched beside one of the cabinets, rearranging pots.

"You're done for the day, Gus," Nash said. "I'll walk you out."

"You running things now?"

That was basically what the former police chief had asked. "Looks like it. Let's go."

The guy walked down the hall and paused briefly to give the twins a disgruntled look.

"See you in the morning, Gus," Betty said, as if today was just another normal day.

Nash locked up after him, then returned to the office. "Give me the names of the guys harassing you."

"Do it, Bernie," Betty said. "I trust Nash."

"I don't," Bernie replied. "He sneaked around in my buildings, after I expressly told him not to."

"I'm part owner with you, and I gave him my permission. And my keys. He didn't sneak anywhere."

Nash glared at him. "Their names, Bernie. Now."

"Travis and Crash. There's another guy—Jed, I think. I don't know their last names."

"Did you sign a contract?" Betty asked.

"No. They recorded me stating the terms of the contract for repayment."

"You have phone numbers?" Nash asked. "How do you contact them?"

Bernie gave Nash two numbers.

Nash texted the numbers and names to Greer. Since he was using the phone Charley gave him, she had that intel too.

"Okay. I'm going to take care of this," Nash said. "Do you two have a safe place to be? A panic room or a tornado shelter? I need you secure when I go into that medical storage room."

The twins looked at each other. "There's Bernie's safe," Betty said.

Nash frowned. "You said to keep clear of that place."

"It used to be a deathtrap," Bernie said. "But after an employee got locked in there and asphyxiated, I made some modifications so that it could be opened from the inside. And I had air holes drilled. We can hide there. We can leave the door open, and if we hear anyone come down to the basement, we can close the door."

"Do that. But just to be safe, text me the combination." Nash sent Greer a text for him and Levi to meet at Bernie's place.

Betty closed her diner for the day, then they walked over to Bernie's store. A few minutes later, Greer and Levi showed up. Bernie let them in. Nash introduced them to the twins.

"Anyone show up on the cameras?" Nash asked.

"Nope. We're clear," Greer said.

Nash turned to Annie. "I need you to go with Betty and Bernie to the safe. Stay there until I get you guys out. At the first sound of anyone moving in the storage room, shut that door." She nodded, but her eyes were huge. It occurred to him that she might have problems with tight spaces. "You okay with that?" What they didn't need was for this to set off a panic attack.

"I'll be fine. I'm just worried about you."

"Geez, thanks," Levi said. "Like we're not capable of taking care of your man."

She shot a look at Nash as she said, "He's not my man."

"Yes, I am," Nash said. "And you don't need to worry about me."

Betty drew her away. When they were inside the safe and the door was nearly closed, Nash turned to his friends and said, "Here's what we're going to do, but we're going to need tools."

"I got tools," Greer replied.

"We have to get into that room in the garage."

"And we have to disable their camera while we do it," Levi said.

Greer nodded. "Yep. Let's go."

They went outside to the alley where he'd parked his

SUV. Lifting the back hatch, he pressed his thumb to a biometric panel. A panel in the cargo floor sprang open to reveal a lighted compartment with enough fire power to handle a week of street fighting.

"Wow. You don't do anything half-assed, do you?" Nash asked.

"They teach you frogs to go half in?" Greer asked.

"We work with what we have where we are." Nash looked at both Levi and Greer. "I just want to make a note that we aren't to wipe the floors up with these guys. My handler wants them alive."

Levi heaved a sigh. "Fuck. It. All. I wasted a trip down here for nothing."

"Whatever," Greer said. "We'll do our best to leave one or two still standing when this is over." From a cubby at one side of the hidden compartment, he took out a pouch and a small black box. "Lockpick and Wi-Fi jammer," he said, smiling.

"Will that mess with the cameras we set up?" Nash asked.

"Nope. Ours run on a licensed, privately owned subfrequency. It's different than what they have in there."

Levi held his hand out. "I'll take the lockpick."

Greer secured his trunk, then they went back into Bernie's basement. Bernie was standing outside the safe, a hand on the door. "I can't hear anything in there."

"Right. We shouldn't be long. Be ready to secure the safe," Nash said.

They went through the connecting basement door, across that building's basement, and into the next building where the garage space with the large steel room was. With light from their phones, Levi was able to unlock the door. When they pulled it open, the room automatically lit up. They walked into a white, sterile, lab-like space. The first two rooms were glass-walled. One was for storage; one had lab equipment. The large room at the back was set up with two hospital beds, two surgical stands, and a full complement of medical monitoring devices for each bed. The overhead lights were ones used in surgical rooms.

"Um, this doesn't look like the storage facility that Bernie thought it was," Levi said.

A chill had gripped Nash ever since they stepped inside that room. He'd been wondering if Harmony Falls was the safe hole-in-the-wall place for the criminals that kept showing up here, or if it was where some of the organ transfers were happening. He had that answer, at least. It was both.

"Fuck," Nash said. *Fuck, fuck, fuck.* Annie was in real danger. "Let's get out of here." They needed to regroup and make a plan. Nash had the impression that Bernie felt there was a deadline approaching. That room had been prepped for an upcoming medical procedure.

He knew who the donor was going to be.

They went back to Bernie's basement room. He was still standing outside the safe. When they first stepped into the room, he jumped for the safe door before realizing who it was.

"You can stand down, Bernie," Nash said.

Annie pushed the heavy door open wider. She came

over to Nash, looking up at him with worried eyes. He rubbed her shoulders. "I'm not gonna lie, babe. It's bad. They have a surgical room pretty much prepped for an operation."

Annie wrapped her arms around her waist. Betty came over to stand beside her.

"We're not going to leave you alone," Nash said. "But I also don't want to spook them. They will just take the transaction elsewhere, transporting you if they have to."

"So how do we persuade them to move forward?" Betty asked.

"Bernie has to kill me," Nash said.

"Oh, no. No," Annie said.

"That's what they said they wanted, but I'm not going to kill you," Bernie said. "I'm not a murderer."

Nash put a hand on the older man's shoulder. "It's not for real. We'll just have to make it look convincing."

"I'm not supposed to see them until two days from now," Bernie said.

"So you'll have good news for them."

"What about Annie?" Betty asked.

"I have to let them take me," she said.

"No," Nash said.

She shook her head. "There's no other way. I'm already tied up in this. I'm why they even have a deal. Without me, their recipient and his broker won't come to town. They're who you're really after."

The room went silent. No one liked her suggestion.

"She's right," Greer said.

"I don't like it," Levi said.

"Does anyone else here have an AB-positive blood type?" Annie asked. No one spoke. "Didn't think so. My blood type is what makes me so valuable to them."

"I can get a profile set up pretty quickly that shows that blood type," Greer said.

"It won't work," Nash said. "The recipient would be suspicious of a donor switch this late in the game."

"Besides, the doctor attending the recipient will conduct his own blood test to be sure the type is right and the donor is healthy." Annie shook her head. "It has to be me."

"I still don't like it," Nash said.

"If I don't help now, I will never be free of them."

"So let's come up with a plan that keeps her protected," Levi said.

Greer nodded. "One of us can always be with her—in an unobtrusive way. I've already cloned her phone, so I can hear her even when she's not on a call."

Annie gave Greer a shocked look. He shrugged and gave her a sheepish grin.

Nash didn't dig into that. "Okay. And Bernie will pretend to shoot me."

"I can take you out and dump you in the death field," Bernie offered.

"The death field?" Levi asked.

"There's a place a few miles outside of town that held murder victims and dead apostates," Greer said. "My wife's mother's body was found there."

Levi shook his head. "You two bastards picked the sickest fucking town to come visit."

"It *was* sick," Betty said. "We cut the cancer out when the cult was ended, now we're trying to survive the chemo, so to speak. We will come out the other side of this." She looked at Nash. "I can make great fake blood."

"And I have a canvas I can wrap over your upper body so you don't have to worry about faking an expression," Bernie said. "I'll kill you here, get you into my car, then drive out to that place."

"Good," Nash replied. "And since we were messing around in their space again, I'm sure you'll be hearing from your friends again soon. They may not wait the two days."

"When do we do this?" Greer asked.

"We'll wait for Bernie's contacts to reach out." Nash reached for Annie's hand. She had the worst assignment in this sting. If everything didn't go exactly as planned, she would be killed. "I'm going to take Annie home. Betty—get that fake blood ready to go. Bernie—find that canvas and rope. Levi and Greer—make sure your tech is working. We don't have an inch of wiggle room with this. And let's recruit Abel to keep an eye on the airstrip. I'm pretty sure he can see it from inside his house."

"Good call. We're on it." Greer looked at Annie. "We're not going to let anything happen to you. Or Nash."

16

Neither Annie nor Nash spoke as he drove them back to the campground. This whole op was insane, he thought, but somehow all the pieces were falling into place. He'd felt so alone when he first left the teams, but he realized that he had a new team he could rely on. Not everyone on it was a battle-hardened warrior, but they had his and each other's backs.

It almost felt as if he belonged to this place, these people, on a path he'd never seen coming.

He was going to be sad when it was time for him to leave.

He drove around the campground, looking for anything that felt hinky. Nothing seemed out of place, so he parked, and they got out. He took Annie's hand and stopped her from going into her cabin. "Not tonight. I need you to stay with me."

She didn't argue. She grabbed her things and followed him.

Inside, Nash looked around his tidy cabin. Where would she be more comfortable? On his bed alone? With him? He decided it was best to let her take the lead. "I'll let you get settled."

She set her stuff on his bed. After taking out a fresh set of underclothes and her toothbrush, she headed for the bathroom. She left the door open as she brushed her teeth. He tried to busy himself in the kitchen, but he was shocked when she turned the shower on and then began to strip. Right there. With the door open. Practically in front of him.

Aw, hell. Was that an invite? Or were they so thoroughly friend-zoned that she felt comfortable stripping around him? Why were women so damned complicated?

He heard the shower door open, but it didn't close.

"Nash—you joining me?"

Fuck. Yeah.

He scrambled to untie his boots, then skipped across the floor as he kicked free of them. He yanked his tee and hoodie off and was dropping his jeans and underwear when he went into the bathroom.

She smiled as she waited for him. When he stepped into the shower, she bit her top lip and looked at his feet.

Shit. His socks. He ripped them off and tossed them out of the shower. She reached for him. He pulled her slim body against his. She was so little in his arms. Six inches shorter, half as wide. But goddamn, her curves. He was already hard. Painfully so. But he didn't want to rush this. He had to go as slow as she needed.

"Wait. I have to get a condom."

Her arms tightened around his neck. "I don't think so. I don't have any STDs. Do you?"

"No."

"I'm on birth control. We're good."

God, he'd get to feel her with nothing between them. Holding her waist, he drew her into the warm stream of water. He bent to nuzzle her neck, the corner of her jaw, before he took her mouth. She was as hungry for this as he was.

He moved his cock between her legs. The difference in their heights let his shaft slip against her sex. Her legs tightened over him. Her eyes were half-lidded, her mouth open, her nostrils flaring as she moved against him. He was so close, but he wasn't going to lose himself before she did.

He pulled away and turned her around, then reached for the soap. He lathered up his hands and rubbed them over her neck, massaging from her shoulder blades up to the base of her skull.

She moaned.

Getting more soap, he ran his hands over her collarbone, chest, and down to her lush breasts. He lingered there, playing with her tight nipples for a moment before moving lower, to her ribs, stomach, hips, and then her sex. She shaved herself so that just a strip of dark hair showed over her mound. Lifting her thigh, he separated her legs and slipped two fingers between her folds. When he felt her body tighten as it readied for an orgasm, he massaged her clit and moved his fingers just the barest way into her. She cried out and gripped his thighs. He wrapped his arm around her waist and held her as she broke free, working his magic over her, extending her pleasure.

When the throes of it eased away, she leaned back against him. He was relieved that she let him hold her in this afterglow moment. She'd rejected him before.

He kissed her temple, the top of her ear, then bent her over the bench and penetrated her. He was big and long, and she was tight and slick. He held her hips as he moved in her, loving the shape of her ass, loving the sight of him sliding in and out.

She arched her back. He could feel little pulses around his cock, precursors to her next orgasm. He reached around and stroked her clit. He was so close. So damned close. But he didn't want to come this way. He pulled free. She cried out in complaint. He turned her around and lifted her, then entered her again. Holding her this way, his arms under her thighs, gripping her ass, was pure heaven.

She held his face and kissed him as the water ran over them. He moved in her, faster, harder, deeper. His whole body tightened. So did hers. She arched against him, her inner muscles gripping him before they both broke free. He groaned as he pumped into her in hot release.

When they were done, he leaned against the cold tile

wall, still holding her, still in her. He didn't want to set her down, didn't want any separation between them. After a moment, he became aware of the little kisses she was placing on his neck, his jaw.

He gripped the back of her head and held her face against his.

He loved her. He was her man.

And he'd be leaving her soon, maybe in just days.

He lifted her off him and set her on her feet. She held his waist and looked up at him, feeling his withdrawal. He was doing now what she'd done the last time they were together.

It was for the best. It was to protect her. And him.

And it hurt like hell.

They finished washing. When they got out, Nash wrapped a towel around her and kissed her forehead. Then, wrapping a towel around his waist, he left the bathroom to give her privacy.

He looked at his phone. Charley was always listening, but the quiet times he got with Annie were just his own. He was going to put it in a drawer, but spoke to his handler instead.

"Night, Charley. Shit's going to hit the fan soon, tomorrow maybe."

Are you prepared? Do you have what you need?

"Yes. Any word on Annie's family?"

Not yet. I want updates tomorrow. And remember, I want them alive, if possible.

"Roger that."

He set the phone in a drawer. Annie came out of the bathroom. He reached for her hand, pausing beside her as they passed in the narrow space. "Stay here, okay?"

"I will."

He brushed his teeth and got ready for bed. When he came out, Annie was in his bed, naked, with the quilt pulled up to her neck. Maybe she wasn't naked. He was just fantasizing. But the outfit she'd worn was still in a heap on the couch. He climbed on the foot of the bed and crawled to the top. When he settled under the covers, he smiled as her warm, nude body curled against his side.

Heaven.

This was it. This was all he'd ever wanted. Right here, right now.

He'd never been so afraid for a mission as he was for the one heading their way. At least they'd have tonight.

"Annie." He tried to stop himself from letting his mouth run, but the words were burning to be freed. "Have you ever thought about having more with someone? Forever, maybe?"

She stroked a few circles over his pec, moving her fingers through the light fur on his chest. "I've never asked for forever from the guys I've been with. I couldn't ask for something I couldn't offer in return."

He squeezed his eyes. Shut up. *Shut. Up.* Don't fucking say it. "But did you want more?"

She pushed herself up on her elbow to look at him. The only light in the cabin was the weak moonlight filtering through the curtains from the window above the bed. "No. Not until now." She kissed the skin beside his nipple. "What about you?"

"Not until now."

She nodded and settled against his side. Neither said anything more. Neither made promises.

They had to get through what was coming first.

NASH'S PHONE RANG. It sounded muted and so far away that he thought it was part of his dream. When the call stopped and started again, he realized his phone was really ringing. He looked at Annie, worried the phone had roused her. She was already wide awake. He got out of bed and went over to the drawer where he'd set Charley's phone, catching it on a ring. It was Greer.

"Yeah."

"It's happening."

"Already?"

"Bernie's friends are in his building, working him over. He's just promised to kill you if they'll spare his sister. They want it done before dawn."

"Good. Let's get this over with. Everything ready?"

"Yep."

"Then it's time to chock up." He hung up. Annie was dressing. He threw on some clothes. In the quiet before the storm, they faced each other. His life would never be the same without her in it.

"Annie Bergen, I lo—"

Quickly, she covered his mouth with her fingers and slowly shook her head. "Don't say it. It will be awful enough if one of us doesn't make it through today, but if I lose the love of my life too, well, I just don't know if I could continue on."

Nash pulled her close and wrapped his arms around her slim shoulders, burying his face in her hair. "You won't be alone today. One of my friends will be near you the whole time."

"And who will be helping you?"

"For my part of the plan, I won't need help. I'll get back to you as soon as I can."

She nodded, then stepped back.

His phone rang. Bernie. He took the call but acted as if he didn't know what was going on in case it was on speaker. "Jesus Christ, Bernie. You know what time it is?"

"I need your help."

"Now? It's the middle of the night."

"Yes. Now. Please. They're threatening Betty. I just —I just can't let them do that."

"Okay. I'm coming over." He hung up.

Annie was breathing in little gasps. He held the back of her neck, forcing her to look at him. "Baby, this is all part of the plan. Keep calm. Go to work like you usually do in a little bit. Greer or Levi will be nearby, though you may not see them. Trust the process. And remember your training. You may need it today."

Nash drove into town and parked in front of Bernie's. Except for some ambient lighting, the store was dark. He tried the door and found it was unlocked. A faint light in the hallway by the offices was coming from the basement.

"Bernie? You here?"

"Down here, Nash."

Nash went down the steps, his gaze sweeping the storeroom for his enemies. He couldn't see them, but Greer had seen them on the cameras. Bernie stepped out from some shelves, keeping one hand still braced there. He was sweating. He looked flushed.

"What's going on, Bernie?"

"I don't—I wouldn't—if it weren't for Betty."

Nash frowned. He really hoped Bernie could hold it together and stick with the plan. These guys needed to be alive to report back to their team that Nash had been eliminated as a threat. If Bernie screwed up, Nash was going to have to take them out, and then the day would be a whole lot harder, if not wrecked completely.

"I'm not following." He gave Bernie a confused look.

Bernie pulled a gun from the shelf. His hand was shaking.

"What are you doing?" Nash asked.

Bernie shook his head. "I don't have a choice." He waved the gun as if to indicate that Nash should walk down the aisle. "Wait, Nash. Put your phone on the shelf. Slowly. Okay, now put your hands up and keep walking. We're going over to the next building."

Nash did so. Bernie pocketed Nash's phone. So far, the old guy was sticking with the plan. Nash hated being on the business end of a gun held by a scared and inexperienced shooter, but he had to have faith.

So far, he hadn't seen Bernie's thugs, but they were here somewhere. He got to the door separating the two buildings. "You don't have to do this, Bernie. You said you wanted me to leave. I'll do that. I'll go. I'll never come back. Shit, my article isn't worth my life."

"It's too late for that. It's you or my sister. I can't let them kill her. She's all I have left in this world."

In the next building over, they passed by one of Bernie's loan sharks. "Turn around, Nash," Bernie said. "I won't shoot you in the back. I owe you that, at least."

Nash slowly turned. His heart was beating like it didn't fit in his chest. Bernie lifted the gun.

"Stop!" a man shouted.

"Travis—" Bernie said, looking confused.

"Jesus, Bernie. You can't do it here." Travis stepped out from behind some shelves. Nash didn't recognize him as anyone he'd seen while investigating Kato's death, but these networks had teams of enforcers. "Crash has the perfect spot out at the death fields. We can't have any evidence here."

"This is ridiculous," Nash said. "You want me gone, I'll go. I like Betty—and Bernie. I don't want anything to happen to them. I'll leave and I won't come back."

"Jed, tie him up." Travis tossed a zip-tie handcuff over to him.

ELAINE LEVINE

Jed yanked one of Nash's hands behind him, but Nash turned and twisted the guy's arm as he tripped him. They scuffled briefly, but Nash landed a punch to Jed's throat, dropping him. Behind them, Nash could hear Travis telling Bernie to hold his fire. Nash pulled Jed's gun from his holster and drew the unconscious guy close as a shield, keeping an arm around his throat. His flesh wouldn't be much of a shield, but Nash had to act the part. He pointed the gun at Bernie.

"Don't shoot!" Travis shouted. "No shooting in here. Geez, you guys. Crash, bring Betty out here."

A third guy came out with Betty in front of him. She'd been crying. She had tape over her mouth, and her hands were bound behind her. Worst of all, Crash had a gun to her head.

Betty screamed into the tape on her mouth. The man shoved her away. He held his pistol on Nash as he came forward.

Travis kept his focus on Nash. "Put your gun down. You can't get out of this." His voice was soft and patronizing.

Nash released Jed and set his gun down, then slowly stood. He held his hands up.

"Bernie—get the cuffs on him and get him out of here. Crash, you're going with them. Make sure it gets done. We've already dug the hole out there. We weren't sure if it would be for Betty or Nash or both, so we made it big enough for any contingency. Remember, Bernie, that your sister may be joining Mr. Thompson if we don't have your complete cooperation."

"Hold on." Bernie went into his storeroom and came back with a canvas tarp and a rope.

"What's that for?" Travis asked.

"I can't look at him when I shoot him. I realized that a moment ago. I'll cover him and then do it. Besides, it'll keep his blood from going everywhere."

17

Annie prepared for work as usual that morning. Nash had told her to keep everything as normal as possible. He wasn't sure how things would go down and didn't want to risk cluing their enemies in on any part of their plan. She looked around for his two friends as she put her backpack and bag in her Jeep, but she didn't see them near their cabins, and on the drive in to work, no headlights followed her.

She parked in the back. She was the first to arrive. It was odd to be there before Betty, but it wasn't quite five a.m. She let herself inside, locking the door behind her. She set her things down in the small lockers near the back door, then headed into the kitchen to make the first pot of coffee for the day. It was the job of whoever got there first to get a brew going so that everyone could have a cup when they arrived.

Gus was in the kitchen, standing just by the doorway, with the lights off. He nearly scared her to death.

She hadn't seen his car outside. She flipped the light on. "What are you doing in the dark, Gus?"

He held up a piece of paper. "Betty left me a list of supplies to get from Bernie. Can you go over with me? I could use a hand."

"Sure." She followed him out the front door and across the street. Bernie's was dark, and the sign read, *Closed*, but the door was unlocked. He must be expecting them. "Bernie?" she called. A light was on in the basement.

Gus looked at his list. "Her note says there would be a few boxes set aside in the basement. Bernie's probably down there pulling her list." He started for the stairs. Annie followed him, despite alarm bells starting to buzz in her head, telling her this was the beginning of the end. Her stomach tightened; she knew what she was walking into. And she'd volunteered to do it. This was the hardest thing she'd ever done. Harder even than running away from the kid farm all those years ago; then, at least, she'd been hopeful of a positive outcome.

"Bernie?" she called out, hoping she was wrong, that this was just an odd day, not an end-of-the-world kind of day. But Bernie didn't answer. Gus walked around, looking for the boxes they were supposed to get. Annie heard a weird, muffled sound coming from beyond the doors that led over to the next building. She went that way and quietly pushed one of the doors open. It was dark inside, but in the glow of light coming from Bernie's basement, she saw something move, and the muffled cries grew louder. Annie grabbed her phone and flipped the flashlight on, then swept it across the room.

Sitting on the floor in a huddle was Betty. Annie rushed over to her. Her hands were tied behind her and tape covered her mouth. "Oh, God. Betty." Annie knelt beside her and eased the tape from her mouth. "What happened?"

Betty's eyes grew wide as she looked at something behind Annie. "Run! Annie, run!"

Before Annie could even turn around, she was grabbed by two men. She tried to free herself, but they had a tight grip on her.

"Secure her," a man said. "I'm going over to the airfield to greet our customer. I want everything ready for when I return."

She looked at him, trying to place where she knew him from. She gasped when it clicked: he was the doctor she'd seen at the diner.

The men dragged her across the dark space into the next building over, the one Bernie had told Nash had a medical storage room. No. God. No.

This was it. This was what they'd come to town to do. And as she'd feared, she was to be the donor. She fought and resisted and dragged her feet. She tripped one guy, but only managed to make him stumble. The other guy wrapped a fist in her hair and yanked her head back.

"Get a needle in her already. Geez, she's hard to handle."

"No sedatives," his buddy said. "No drugs. She needs to be clean. We need all of her."

They managed to get her into the special medical room. The light was blindingly bright. There were two rooms at the front, cubbies, really, both with glass walls. One housed supplies. The other looked to be some sort of lab. Beyond that was a wide-open room with special surgical lights. There were two gurneys—one with restraints. There were also two trays of sterile implements, a couple of stools, and a full complement of medical monitors and cuffs.

The guys dragged her over to the gurney with the straps, but as they tried to wrestle her down, she kicked the bed away, then kicked the tray of surgical tools. One of the men let her go as he scrambled to set everything right again. She struggled to free herself from the other guy, but his grip was too tight. She only managed to swing around in front of him, but that was all the latitude she needed. She kicked his knee with the side of her foot, then slammed her knee into his chin when he bent over in pain, gaining her release. She scrambled back a few feet but wasn't ready for the fist that hit her jaw. The blow threw her to the ground, over the cold steel tools.

She scrambled backward, then realized she was crawling over sharp things. She grabbed a scalpel and held it, blade flat, against her wrist. Nash had told her the best places to strike an opponent and that when a confrontation devolved to a fight, death was the only desirable outcome—and preferably not hers. She knew she had to make a slice against his neck or his groin, but it might be harder to succeed with a cut through his jeans. The other option was to shove the knife right into his eye.

It was him or her.

Afterward, she would take care of the other one. And then she was going to lay waste to the whole fucking room.

The guy yanked her to her feet, his hands under her arms. She didn't think twice, didn't hesitate, didn't give any airtime between her conscience and what she had to do. She flipped the scalpel forward and stabbed it through his eye and all the way to the back of his skull. His shocked body didn't immediately release her. It was odd. He stood there, gripping her in his dead hands as the light went out of his other eye.

He fell on top of her, dropping them both to the ground. Blood was pouring out of him, all over her and the floor. She cried as she struggled to get out from under him. The other guy had regained consciousness and stumbled toward her just as she got free.

She grabbed the metal tray the tools had been on and slammed it into his neck, then used the edge to hit his head, dropping him again.

It was done. She was safe.

For now.

But how to hold off others coming in? She rushed over to the door and set the lock, but she knew that wouldn't hold for long. Someone out there had to have the key. She thought about trying to build a blockade, but that also wouldn't hold.

Was it smart to stay in there? Was it safe to leave? Was there a brief window of time where she could break free and exit the building? Where was Nash? Where were his friends?

She doused the lights in the room, then cracked the door just a fraction. She couldn't see anyone through that sliver, but that didn't mean there wasn't someone in the garage—or just outside of it—posted as a guard. She opened the door wider and popped her head out. A light was on in the next building over, one building down from Bernie's. She heard men talking in there. Sounded as if they were headed her way.

She closed and locked the door, then moved away from it. In the darkness, she stumbled over something on the floor. Maybe a barricade wouldn't stop anyone from entering, but it would slow them down and take their attention off her—perhaps long enough that she could get a shot in.

She went back into the big surgical room and took the guns from the guys on the floor, then found a set of plastic handcuffs in the back pocket of the dead one. She dragged the one who was still alive over to a table in the corner and wrapped his arms around its leg, close to the lower shelf, then pulled the tie tight. He might regain consciousness, and with it his mobility, but it would be difficult for him to get around tied to a table.

She prayed Nash and his guys would get to her soon. She knew they were waiting for all the pieces to fall into place so that they could make the most damage to the trafficking ring, but there was a fine line between beating the bad guys and surviving this event. She didn't know quite where that line was. Her training with Nash had helped her so far, but how long would her luck hold out?

It was best to not dwell on that and instead turn her focus to doing everything she could to give him and his friends the time they needed while she took care of her own survival. It helped knowing that one of his friends had to be nearby, had to have seen her brought into this room.

In the lab, she found an under-cabinet light. It helped her see but wasn't bright enough to illuminate all the hiding spots. She turned the gurneys on their sides and made a V shape, interlocking the legs somewhat. She had no idea how much protection they would be from bullets, but it was her best option.

Next, she went into the two anterooms and pulled anything on wheels—tables, chairs, cabinets, any and all of it, and clogged up the entry, jamming pieces where she could. It wouldn't stop anyone for long, but every minute she could reclaim might be the ticket to her survival. Really, the only thing she had going for her at the moment was the fact that her captors didn't want to hurt her body and thereby ruin her valuable organs.

Situated where she was, she could get the drop on anyone who came through that door. Might not be for long, but she'd go down fighting.

NASH AND BERNIE sat in the back seat of the SUV that was bouncing along the moonlit dirt road. Nash avoided looking at Betty's brother, didn't want him to break his act by trying to whisper or wink or in any way undermine his role.

It took a while to drive out to the killing field. The road wasn't the best. Nash knew he could take out the two in the front seat, but Charley wanted them alive. And they each needed to do what was expected of them —or there would be collateral damage. These thugs needed to witness his death and report in when the deed was done. There were ways around that. His biggest concern right now was keeping Bernie calm. At least he was holding the gun without his finger on the trigger.

Nash couldn't say the same for the guy in the passenger seat up front. He was half turned toward them, his pistol pointed at Bernie. He did have his finger on the trigger.

The SUV turned off the larger dirt road onto an even rougher one. After a while, it came to a stop. The guy in the passenger seat said, "Let's go, you two."

A cold wind hit them as they walked over to a pile of dirt beside a freshly dug hole. Nash looked back at the car and saw the driver standing behind his opened door, pointing his gun toward them.

"I don't know how to do this," Bernie said.

"It ain't rocket science, Bernie. Back him up to the hole and plant one in his chest."

Nash held his hands in front of him as if pleading to be spared. In one step, he twisted the gun out of Bernie's hands then pivoted and shot the knee of the guy standing with them. He pushed Bernie to the ground and checked the driver, but Greer was already securing him. Geez, that guy was like a ghost. Nash supposed Greer had come out earlier and knew where to situate himself based on the fresh hole, but that, still, was a wild bit of luck.

The guy whose knee Nash had just blown out was losing a lot of blood. The shock of the blow had dropped him to the ground, bouncing the gun from his hand. He was trying to crawl over to it. Nash stepped on the gun. "Bernie—get over here and cut me free."

Bernie looked around fearfully, then used his pocketknife to cut him loose. Nash retrieved the gun and tucked it at his back. Greer tossed him a zip-tie, and Nash secured the man.

"Any updates on the plane?" Nash asked Greer.

"None, but there's no reception out here." He tossed his keys to Nash. "Get outta here. Bernie and I will take care of these two."

Bernie handed Nash his phone back.

Nash nodded to the guy he'd shot. "That one needs a tourniquet. My team wants them alive. These two are expected to report in when they get back into range."

He jogged over to Greer's SUV, which was parked nearby behind a rock outcropping, and rushed away from the killing fields. He checked his phone a few times, but he didn't have cell reception. Messages flooded his phone as he came into town. One stood out. It was from Abel. A flight had landed at the airfield. That was ten minutes earlier.

Shit.

He parked out front of Bernie's store and shot a text over to Greer to secure the airfield, that a plane had already come in. Damn, he hoped Greer was already back in cell phone range. Abel could observe the plane from the safety of his B&B, but he was not a fighter. Sending him out there would be his death.

A text came in from Levi. Annie was in the special surgery two buildings from Bernie's. The convoy from the airport was arriving down below.

Nash went inside Bernie's store. All was quiet. He headed down the hallway toward the basement stairs when Betty's cook stepped out of the office. Nash slipped behind a corner at the entry to the hall, barely missing Gus' gunfire.

"I brought your girl over here for her special appointment. She was like a lamb to slaughter."

"You think you're going to make it out of this alive?"

"Odds are ten to one in my favor."

"I'll take those odds." Nash knelt and leaned around the corner, shooting toward Gus.

Gus popped back into Bernie's office. Anticipating Nash's movement, he started firing through the wall. Nash stayed put and held his fire until Gus stepped out of the office. One gut shot took him down. Before Nash could get close enough, two more guys came into the hallway from the stairs. Nash picked them both off with nonlethal strikes. It was really pissing him off leaving any of these fools alive, but on the off chance that Charley's group could get any useful info out of them, he supposed it was worth it. This trafficking ring had to be stopped, no matter how far its tendrils ran.

Nash went back into Bernie's store and locked the front door. The sun was up now. He did not want shoppers stumbling in on what was happening. He found some twine in the narrow hardware section. Cutting the pack open, he freed a few feet.

Gus was getting to his feet when Nash got to the office. He kicked Gus in the gut, then pushed his gun away. Kneeling on Gus' back, Nash bound his hands behind him. He took Gus' gun, then tied up the other two guys as well.

Damn, they were lucky he had no-kill orders.

Shooting had started below. Nash collected the other two guns, then went down the stairs. No telling if there was another shooter down there waiting to pick him off. The lights were off, keeping the storeroom dark. He stepped beside a shelf and paused to listen to the room. It was silent. Shooting was still happening one building over. He set all but one gun on a shelf before heading that way.

Nash went down the aisle then turned the corner and went up the next. There was a body lying across the way. He checked for a pulse, but the guy was gone. He knelt and looked through the open stock shelves to see if anyone else was in the room. Maybe Levi had already cleared it.

Cautiously, he crept forward to the end of that aisle. A shadow shifted. There was movement coming toward him. A hand with a gun came around the corner. Nash grabbed it and yanked the man forward. His gun went off as Nash shoved the guy's head into the metal shelf, dropping him. Nash kicked that gun away then continued on, meeting no one else in Bernie's storeroom.

The next section he had to clear—and cross—was the empty space in the building next to Bernie's, between the grocery and the old medical building. Without night-vision goggles, it was impossible for him to see if anyone was in that big space. The only way he could get to Levi—and Annie—was through that room.

He remembered where some crates and boxes were stacked from his time in there earlier that morning. He ran from the door to the first of those without incident. The shooting had stopped in the medical building. He had no idea if that was good or bad. Levi had been on his own with at least half a dozen bad guys escorting the organ recipient.

Nash worked his way over to the open doorway. Greer texted to let him know the airfield had been secured.

Nash took a quick look around to assess the situation. There was a white cargo van with its back doors open toward the medical vault. Those doors were peppered with holes. Three bodies were down on Nash's side of the van. He bolted for the van, then did a quick check to see if anyone was in the back. It was empty.

The van was set up as an ambulance, with a bench and compartments on both walls.

Where was the transplant recipient? Where was Levi?

He couldn't tell from where he was if anyone was in the front cab. He moved forward along the side of the van. The second he looked in the window, he realized he was staring at a gun barrel. He pulled back. The driver opened the door enough to slip his gun out and start randomly shooting. Nash crouched and ran forward, grabbing the gun and the guy's hand and yanking him out of the van. He shot the man's right shoulder as he stood over him, then kicked his gun away.

Another quick check of the front cab showed it was empty.

"Nash," Levi shouted. "Two more outside." His friend jumped into the passenger seat. "Get in and punch it!"

Nash gunned the accelerator just as one of the remaining guys stepped in front of the van. He was run down. More shots sounded as Levi took out the guy on that side of the garage door.

"That it?" Nash asked.

"I lost count. You hear back from Greer?"

"He's got the airfield secured. Where's Annie?"

"Still in the medical vault. I think. I haven't been able to get in there, and I haven't seen her come out."

Nash jogged back into the medical building, Levi close behind him. The door to the vault was open. A guy was inside talking to Annie. Nash knew that voice.

It belonged to the former police chief, Gavin Erickson.

ANNIE HAD HAD some time after she first locked herself in the vault to think through a better strategy for when the harvesters got into the room. She dragged the gurneys over to a corner and set them up on their ends, making a tall fortress. She'd sat in there for a while, before she realized that was the perfect hiding spot and would be the first target of anyone who came in.

Leaving the upended gurneys in place, she went into the storage section of the front rooms and pushed one of the steel cabinets off the wall slightly. As torn up as the entire space was, the cabinet being out of place wouldn't seem odd.

She got in her hiding space behind it and waited. Seemed like a long time passed. God, what was happening? She couldn't hear a thing. Where was Nash? Was he safe? Were his friends safe?

She could feel the onset of one of her panic attacks. She pulled her shirt up to cover her nose and mouth, pretending she was with Nash, somewhere safe, looking into his dark blue eyes as he bent close and ordered her to breathe with him, slowly, slowly.

A tear spilled down her cheek.

Were any of them going to get out of this? If this trafficking ring did have international origins, a showdown here in this little town might barely be a ripple in their larger network.

She heard the door unlock.

It was time.

She reminded herself not to take the first shot—it might be Nash coming for her.

Someone cursed as the door banged into her blockade. She heard things getting shoved out of the way. Then someone was in the hallway. She was afraid to peek out of her hiding place to see who it was. But she had a terrible feeling that it wasn't Nash or any of his friends—they would announce themselves to her.

The person climbed over the clutter. The beam of his flashlight swept the room. He cussed, probably when he saw the two men she'd left in the big room.

"Annie. Annie, girl."

She knew that voice. Gavin. She squeezed her eyes shut. If he was in here, then Nash hadn't made it. She was on her own now. She had to keep still and keep quiet. She didn't know how many more would be coming in with him.

He'd moved into the main surgery. She was closer to the door than he was. Could she make a dash for it?

"Annie. You don't have to be afraid of me. You know me. I helped you before. I'm not angry about the fire at your old home. I don't think you did it anymore. You can come out. It's a big mess in here. You've dug a deep hole for yourself, but I can help you deal with this."

She jumped when he knocked down her gurneys and cursed.

"I see you're a murderer now. I would not have expected that from you, little Annie. Or should I call you Sarah? Which is the real you?" His voice was sickeningly sweet, as if he were placating a child. The way he said terrible things with that soft voice gave her chills.

He was coming over to the front rooms—she could tell by the way his flashlight moved. He went into the lab area first. Then his light spilled through the cracks into her hiding place. He knew where she was.

She stepped out of her hiding place, holding the gun she'd taken from one of the guys. He was holding a gun on her as well, but his flashlight blinded her. She stepped back behind her cabinet. The way she'd positioned it, she'd given herself a sight line between the cabinet and the wall. When he shot at her, he hit the cabinet. The bullet pierced the metal and ricocheted before stopping.

She didn't wait for the sound to stop. She aimed at where she'd seen his gun fire. She heard him go down, but had she hit him? Was he down for good? His flashlight was on the floor. Since it wasn't pointing at her, it just gave a soft glow to the room.

He was unmoving on the floor.

She cautiously crept away from her hiding spot toward him. When she was standing over him, he smiled and raised his arm. She emptied her clip into him.

When the roar of her assault eased away, there was movement at the door to the vault. Dammit. She'd gone through her firepower. She pointed her empty gun at whoever it was anyway.

"Annie? It's me. Nash. I'm coming in, okay? It's just me. Please don't shoot me."

Relief made the air rush out of her lungs. She couldn't quite get a full breath to replace it, so she began gasping for air. And then his arms were around her. He brought her in close to him. She pulled back to check him out, running her hands over his face, his body, his arms. He was whole. He was okay.

The light flipped on in the room. Levi joined them. "You okay, Annie?" he asked, a hand on her shoulder.

"I am now. I killed him. That felt good."

Nash laughed.

"You killed all of them," Levi said after a brief walk through the surgery. "Jesus, Nash, you got yourself a fighter."

"Best kind of woman there is." Nash laughed.

"Are we safe?" Annie asked.

Nash took a long breath. It felt like a negative answer.

"You're safe," came a woman's voice.

All three of them turned to look at her. She was a slim blond with an air of authority.

"Charley, I presume?" Nash said.

"I am." They shook hands. He introduced Charley to Levi and her.

"Greer—is he good?" Nash asked.

"He's good. We've secured all three sites of this showdown. We recovered the recipient and his staff in the alley behind the building. It's over, but you'll all need to be debriefed."

Annie wrapped an arm around Nash's waist. "What's happening? Who is she?"

"She's why I came here. You and this"—he gestured around the room—"are why she sent me here."

"Your efforts to take down this trafficking ring, Ms. Bergen, are very much appreciated," Charley said. "You helped us close an investigation that's been in the works for over a decade."

Annie looked up at Nash. "I killed people here."

"In self-defense," he said. "Let's talk to Charley and her people. We'll figure this out."

"Don't worry, Annie," Levi said as he followed them out of the room. "There's always a post-action debrief."

"And then beer," Nash said.

"I don't drink," Annie said.

"Then water. We'll have a round of waters," Nash said, laughing.

"Might even have two rounds." Levi chuckled.

They stepped out of the secure medical suite and into the garage. Betty was there, with her brother. She looked a wreck. Her mouth had an angry red mark over it where the tape had been. Her eyes were swollen from crying, and her face was pale from the stress.

She came forward and hugged Annie, rocking her slightly as she patted her back. "I'm so glad you're alive."

Annie started to cry. "I'm glad you're all right too."

When Betty stepped back, Bernie was there, looking

very much in need of a hug as well. She smiled at him and waved him closer. These two were like a real aunt and uncle to her. She stepped back and wiped the tears from her face.

"Oh my God." She grabbed Nash's arm. "Gus. He's one of them. He lured me over here."

"He is one of them. And Charley has him in custody," Nash said.

"The doctor was here, too," Betty said.

"He's also in our custody," Charley said.

"So it's done?" Annie asked Nash. "All of it? Did you get your answers too?"

He shook his head. "Your end of things is done. I'm still waiting to see if there's any connection between my friend's death and this trafficking ring. I'm hopeful there is, else Charley would not have sent me out here."

Annie took his hand and smiled up at him. "I'm glad she did."

18

"I can't believe it's over." Annie propped her arm on his chest and braced her chin on it as she looked at him.

Nash gave her a smile he wasn't quite feeling. Some of it was over. Now they had to decide what was next. His old phone buzzed. He'd quit using Charley's phone. A cold fist settled in his gut as he got up to get the text.

It was his former master chief, summoning him back to the base in Virginia.

"What is it?" Annie asked.

Nash sat on the edge of the bed. "I have to go back."

She came over and wrapped her arms around him. She kissed his shoulder. "Okay. When are you leaving?"

"I guess this morning. The FBI are still in town, cleaning up the mess the traffickers left. Some of them are staying in these cabins. You'll be safe, but if you'd rather go stay with Abel, I'll make a call."

"I'll be fine here. If I get nervous, I'll reach out to Abel."

"And call me. You have my real number now."

"I do." She smiled at him, but her eyes were sad. "I don't want to go."

"You have to finish what you started. I learned that through all of this."

NASH DROVE to the main gate at the base. He recognized the guard on duty, but the guy just nodded at him as if he were a stranger. Nash gave him his ID and info and then was ordered to park and wait for an escort.

This summons was beginning to feel like a perp walk.

A Jeep rolled up, stopping in front of his truck. "Mr. Thompson?" Nash nodded. "We'll take you to Captain Bradley."

Nash got in the back. They drove to the building Nash had last left in his walk of shame. They parked, then both escorts got out to walk him into the building. They paused outside the captain's office, while one of his escorts announced his arrival.

He'd been away from all such formalities in the last month. Funny how quickly he'd acclimated to civilian life. When he was granted an audience, he walked into a room with three of his former senior officers. His first instinct, despite his month of civilian life, was to salute.

Fortunately, he resisted that reaction. These three had seen to his other-than-honorable discharge. He didn't owe them fuck.

Captain Bradley stood. "Chief Petty Officer Thompson, on behalf of a grateful nation, we've asked you here today to restore you to your former position on the teams, with all due back pay, accrued retirement, and earned honors. Your record over the last month will reflect the special assignment you undertook on behalf of the Department of Homeland Security while on a sabbatical from your post. Your efforts have helped put an end to a ring of organ thieves who were attacking both our wounded personnel and harming civilians as well. You did this at great cost to your personal safety, working without the benefit of a team, and with honor that was over and above any high expectation this office held on your behalf."

Nash was confused. "I don't understand."

"We believed in the work you were doing for Kato," Commander Cochran said. "The only problem was that your investigation couldn't go where it needed to while you were an active member of the Navy."

"And your anger and reaction to your severance needed to be believable, even to your own team," Master Chief Boutell said. He held out his hand. "You're back."

"And if I choose not to return to duty?" Nash asked. The question stunned the room into a moment of silence.

"We've considered that option′ and have prepared your exit papers. We can shred them, or you can sign and submit them," Captain Bradley said. "For the sake of the Navy, I hope you choose to stay."

"Take a few days to decide," the master chief said as he handed Nash his Navy ID and the keys to his old apartment. Nash stared at them. It was as if none of the last month had happened. As if he'd never met Annie, never encountered a brave little town trying to find its feet again.

But that time had happened, and it had changed him. He'd seen the other side. As a SEAL, the only thing he'd feared was losing a brother...and leaving the teams. But now he had a whole lot more to fear, like losing the woman of his dreams and the chance of a lifetime—a chance to make a difference and have a life after his career in special operations warfare.

On the drive to his old apartment, Nash felt like his heart had already made its decision and was waiting for his head to catch up. He parked at his apartment complex. Everything was just as it had been a month ago. Everything was the same, except him. He unlocked his apartment door and immediately felt a presence inside. Maybe it was the faint hint of an unfamiliar perfume.

A woman was sitting in his living room. "Nash," she said.

Even though she sat silhouetted by the window, that silky voice was a dead giveaway. "Charley."

"You did good. I'm glad you were reinstated."

He said nothing. How did she know that he had been reinstated? Unless she'd had a hand in it? "Was the Colorado group connected to the one operating here?"

"Yes. The good doctor, Roger Mason, was the same surgeon who operated on your friend. He had a slew of false credentials and identities."

"What happened to the organ recipient?"

"He, his doctors, brokers, and guards are in our custody. We are learning a good bit from them that's filling in some blanks for us."

She stood and handed him a bank card. "Your fee."

"I had help from Greer and Levi."

"I've compensated Owen for Greer's time, and paid Levi for his." She smiled. "I appreciate the intro to other skilled operators."

Nash didn't know if that was a good thing. He didn't take the card. "I didn't do it for the money. I did it for my friend." *And my woman*, he added to himself.

Charley tossed the card on his coffee table. "It's yours. What you do with it is your business. Save it. Spend it. Toss it away. I don't care." She walked to the door but paused before leaving. "You're at one of those points in life that changes everything. Make the right choice. And keep our phone—we may be calling upon you again."

"You can call. I may or may not answer."

"As expected." She reached for the door handle, but again paused. She took a folded envelope out of her big purse. "We found Annie's family."

Nash felt dizzy suddenly. That was the single most important thing to Annie. Finding her family. Who were they? Did they miss her still? Did they even think of her anymore?

"Where are they?" he asked as he took the packet.

"Colorado."

Shit. She'd lived in the same state as her family her whole life and never knew it. Life was sickening sometimes. All that wasted time.

He didn't want to waste any more of it—not in his life, not in hers.

"You served honorably," Charley said, "but a wise man knows when one phase has ended and another's begun."

She left his apartment, but the faint scent she wore lingered. He missed Annie, missed the way she smelled, the way she smiled, the way he felt when she turned the full force of her ice-blue gaze on him.

He sat on the sofa and stared at the packet and the bank card. What if her people were criminals? Or dead. Or...

There was only one way to find out. He opened the packet. It hadn't been sealed, just pinned closed with metal tines. He unfolded the papers. Each held a brief dossier with information on her parents and sister— their names, jobs, hobbies, addresses. They were still alive, still married, still a family. Stapled to each page was a photo. Annie was a younger version of her mom.

Nash picked up his phone and hit a speed dial button to call his master chief. He picked up on the first ring. "Go, Nash."

Nash didn't speak. Boutell had always answered the

phone that way, but right now, it felt as if he were saying what Nash had called to tell him he'd be doing.

"I mean it. You should go," Boutell said.

"You don't even know where I was."

"You think we weren't keeping tabs on you?"

"Were you working with Charley?"

"In a loose capacity. She had charge of our asset — you. I know you felt adrift without your team, but we would have been there fast if you'd needed us."

"I have to go back."

"I get it. I'd go too. We'll overnight your exit papers when you get where you're going. Fair winds, my friend. I may pop in to see you."

"I hope you do. Harmony Falls needs a new police department."

NASH MADE one more stop before leaving town.

Kato was a local boy, and his parents still lived in the area. They'd helped Nash in the early days of his investigation into what had happened to their son. They deserved an update.

He parked out front of their house in Virginia Beach. The bright, sunny day did not match his mood. His investigation had brought to light a dark side of humanity. He wrestled with how much of that to tell Kato's family as he walked to their porch.

Kato's dad yanked the door open after the first knock. "Nash," he said.

"Mr. Baldean."

"Come in." Kato's dad stepped back, holding the door wide open.

"I wanted to give you an update on...things."

"Sure. Want some coffee?"

"I'd like that."

Kato's mom stepped out of the kitchen, a dish towel in her hands. She gasped when she saw Nash, then hurried over. She gave him a hug, then leaned back to look at him. "Come in the kitchen. I'll put a pot on."

They sat at the kitchen table.

"Whatever it is, son, go ahead and say it," Mr. Baldean said.

Nash looked at Kato's parents. "My search for the people involved in illegally harvesting Kato's kidney took me to a small town in Colorado. It seemed an unlikely place to find anything, but I learned the organ network was operating there and was even building up an infrastructure so that they could keep their illegal work going."

"Did you stop them?" Mrs. Baldean asked as she sat at the table.

"Yes." Nash drew a long breath. "I don't know if it made much more than a dent in the flow of illegal organs, but we stopped one network. Those involved will be held accountable."

"I want to go to their trials," Mr. Baldean said.

"I'll send you info on that when I have it," Nash said. "There's something else. I should have said this before." He stared at the table, too much of a coward to look at their expressions. The room took on a strained silence. "I'm why your son was wounded. We were in a small convoy following Afghan soldiers to a location where we hoped to capture an ISIS leader. The vehicle in front of us hit an IED. The explosion flipped our Humvee. I was ejected in the middle of the street. It was an ambush; our enemies were waiting for us. A gunfight ensued. I started to rouse in the middle of it. Kato risked himself to pull me out of danger." Nash finally looked at Kato's parents. "He saved my life."

Mrs. Baldean started to weep. Her husband gripped her shoulder. "Thank you for telling us," he said.

Nash could barely breathe as he waited for them to kick him out of their house. *Fuck that.* He lurched to his feet and backed away from the table. He had to get out of there.

Mrs. Baldean stood.

"I'm so sorry," Nash said. "I'm why your son died." He pivoted to leave, but he felt a hand on his back. Kato's mom was standing behind him.

"You aren't why he died," she said. "He was on his way to a full recovery before the harvesters got him. You did not do that."

Mr. Baldean stood, offering him a sad smile. "We miss our boy something fierce, Nash. But we do not blame you. And you should not blame yourself. Kato loved you. He loved all of you boys."

Nash clenched his jaw.

"And he died a double hero," Mrs. Baldean said, smiling through tears. "He saved you and helped you stop that ring of criminals. I am so very proud of him. And you." She reached for Nash. He gave her a tight hug.

When Nash looked at Mr. Baldean, the man gave him a nod. "Let's have that coffee now."

NASH PARKED behind the diner in Harmony Falls. He felt an odd mix of excitement, exhaustion, and fear. The info he held in his hands might mean the end of his time with Annie. It certainly would be a new beginning for her.

His phone rang. "Nash?" Annie said.

"Yeah."

"Hi."

"Hi." He leaned against his truck.

"I don't mean to bother you...I just needed to hear your voice, see how things went."

"Good, I think. And I love hearing your voice. Hey. There's something outside the back door. A surprise."

"I don't like surprises, Nash."

"Babe, you'll like this one. Don't hang up. I want to be with you when you see it."

"Okay." Seconds later, she came outside. She stopped in her tracks when she saw him. "You're here," she said into her phone.

He set his down on his hood and opened his arms. Before he could even acknowledge his fear that she wouldn't come to him, she was in his arms.

"You're back." She leaned away so she could look up at him. "Why? I didn't think you were going to come back."

"It's kinda hard to be away from my heart." He kissed her, long and hard. "I have some news for you. Good news."

She watched him expectantly. He handed her the papers. "My people found your family."

Her hands shook as she unfolded the sheets and stared at them.

"Your folks seem to be good people," Nash said. "You feared they were who sold you to the traffickers, but that's not what happened."

Annie was quiet as she made a first pass over the papers. "They're still alive. Justin and Vicki Ross. And I have an older sister named Brielle. Bree, they call her." She hugged him. He heard a muffled giggle against his chest. She looked up at him with happy eyes, her face showing her shock and joy. "My real name is Annie Ross." She looked at him with a strange expression. "I chose the name Annie when I was in foster care. I picked my real name. And I'm a year older than I thought I was."

A year closer to his age, although, if that single year mattered, then so did the remaining nine that separated them.

"I have to tell Betty. I want to go see them." She spun around and headed for the door. He waited by his truck, trying to figure out how much of this she wanted to do by herself, and how much she wanted to include him in. "Nash, come on! I can't wait to tell Betty."

Betty was in her office when Annie burst inside. "I found them! They're still alive! Well, actually, Nash found them, but they're real."

Betty turned from her desk. "Um, what?"

Annie hugged her, waving the papers in her face. "My parents. My family. Look! They're right here in Colorado." She handed the papers to Betty.

The older woman looked through them. "Well, you have to go. You have to go meet them."

Annie nodded. She was standing on her tiptoes and flapping her hands, wearing a smile that showed two rows of her pretty teeth.

Nash had seen her withdrawn, anxious, panicked, fearful, passionate, but this was entirely new. He'd never seen her so joyful. Like a piece of her soul had instantly healed.

Christ Almighty, he hoped her parents were good people.

Annie looked at him. "When do we leave?"

We. She wanted him with her.

"By the looks of your man's face," Betty said, "he could use some sleep first."

Nash nodded. "It's true. I've driven halfway across the country and back in three days. Give me a few hours' sleep."

"You mind losing me for a while?" Annie asked Betty.

"We'll be fine here until you come back, which I hope you will."

Annie nodded. "You've been wonderful to us, Betty."

Betty stood and hugged them both. "Get outta here. Go figure out your next steps." She held Nash's hands a long moment. "Thank you for all you did for Harmony Falls. With that gang gone, we might have a fighting chance. You know you're welcome back at any time." She reached for Annie's hand too. "Both of you."

Nash kissed her cheek. "Thanks. I'll remember that. You'll let Bernie know, yeah?"

"Oh yeah. And he'll tell the whole town." She laughed.

They walked outside. At their cars, Annie paused. "What now?"

"Let's go back to the cabin. I think you should phone your parents. This is a big surprise for them as well. There's no point rushing out to see them if they're out of town."

"Okay. Good point. See you back at the cabin."

NASH'S CABIN was too small to house a caged tiger, he decided as he watched Annie pace from one end to the other and back.

"Come sit here with me," Nash said, patting the space next to him on the bed. "We'll call your folks and see how things are."

Annie was looking pale, just inches away from a full-on panic.

"Bring your phone and their number. Let's just break the ice. They'll be as surprised as you were."

She grabbed both and settled next to him.

"Comfortable?"

"No."

"That's okay. This is exciting. Hand me your phone." He punched in the numbers then put it on speaker. When it rang, he handed it to her.

"Hello?" It was a woman's voice.

"Hi. Um. Is this Vicki Ross?" Annie asked.

"It is. Who's calling?"

Annie gave him a wide-eyed, frightened look. He nodded at her to continue.

"My name is Annie Bergen. I-I'm your daughter."

"No. No, it's not true. Stop calling us. This is cruel. I have your number, and I'm going to give it to the police."

They heard a distant voice come closer to the phone. "Who is it, honey?"

"It's them again. Pretending to be our Annie." The woman could be heard crying.

"Hello? Who is this?"

"I'm Annie. Your daughter."

Silence.

Nash wondered who'd been calling them pretending to be Annie. Had that happened recently? Could it be the gang they just shut down had been trying to see if Annie had gone back home?

Nash leaned close. "Mr. Ross, this is Nash Thompson. I'm your daughter's boyfriend. We've compared her DNA to yours and your wife's. She is an exact match. She is your daughter."

"I don't believe you. Send us a picture."

Nash snapped the pic and sent it while they were still connected. There were some rustling noises while they handled the phone and flipped to the text. Next came a loud scream. As soon as that ended, they could hear sobbing.

"Annie?" her mom said. "Is it really you?"

"It's me."

"Where are you, honey? Just tell us. We'll come get you. Are you safe?"

"I'm safe. I'm in Harmony Falls. We're coming to see you in the morning."

"Mr. Ross, Mrs. Ross—I don't want you driving in shock," Nash said. "We'll come to you. You have Annie's number. Call her anytime."

"Okay. God. I can't wait. We can't wait," her dad said. "Do you know where we live? How did you get our number? I know that wasn't given out on the DNA sites."

"We had a private investigator find you," Nash said.

"Annie, honey, this is Mom. Baby, I need to hear your voice."

"Hi, Mom. I'm here. I'll be home soon." Annie's voice broke on a sob. "I can't wait to meet you both. And Bree."

"Honey, I know we're strangers to you, but you

aren't a stranger to us," her mom said. "We never gave up hope. We always kept you in our hearts and in our prayers."

Annie cried. Her sniffle was her answer.

Nash finished the call. "Thank you both. We'll be there tomorrow."

"Text us when you leave," her dad said.

"We will. See you soon."

Annie wrapped her arms around his neck and buried her face against his skin. "I hope they like me. I'm not the little girl they lost."

"Of course not. You're a grown woman now."

"I killed people."

"Yeah, I think that's something we don't need to talk about with them. Just tell them you defended yourself, if it comes up, and you survived. None of that's a lie."

She nodded, laughing as she looked up at him, crying and smiling simultaneously.

———

19

Grand Junction, Colorado, was a stunning mountain town—red brick buildings dating from the late 1800s nestled at the base of the Grand Mesa. It was a colorful and bustling place, even that late in the season.

"It's beautiful," Annie said.

"Do you remember any of this?"

She shook her head.

The drove out of town to her parents' house, a mid-century rambler a little way outside of town. It had snowed recently, so patches of white dotted the ground.

They pulled into her parents' driveway. He shut the engine off. They both sat there a long moment, preparing for what was coming.

She sent him a worried look.

"They sounded nice on the phone," Nash said.

"They did."

"Nice like you."

"You think?"

He nodded. "They're probably dying to see you. Why don't we get this started?"

The front door opened as they approached. A burly black lab came running out to greet them. He bashed Annie with his tail, which made her laugh. When she looked up, her mom and dad were standing on the front stoop.

Something twisted in her gut. Every memory she'd ever lived began shouting at her, and the focus overload gave her a welcome numbness. This would be great, or it wouldn't, but either way, she would be fine.

Her mom had straight silver hair cut in a shoulder-length bob. The lines on her face had stories to tell. Her crystalline blue eyes were a mirror image of Annie's. She had on a soft blue sweater that she wore with jeans.

Annie's dad wasn't as tall as Nash, nor as bulky. He had warm brown eyes and salt-and-pepper hair cut short. He was wearing a fleece vest over a tee and a Henley and a regular pair of jeans.

She'd played this very moment so often in her mind, but now that it was happening, she had no idea how to proceed. Her parents smiled at them but waited for her to approach. Her mom was gripping and releasing her own hands nervously.

Annie straightened her shoulders, lifted her head, and moved closer. "Hi. I'm Annie."

Her mom stifled a sob as her dad came forward. "Welcome home, Annie. We're your parents—I'm

Justin, and your mom's Vicki, but you know that
already."

Annie drew a ragged breath as she nodded. The
Rosses. That was what their background papers had
said. She was Annie Ross. Still, she just stood there,
frozen.

Nash reached around her to shake hands with her
dad. "I'm Nash Thompson. It's nice to meet you, Mr.
and Mrs. Ross."

"Thank you for bringing our daughter home."

"My pleasure." Nash gave Annie an encouraging
smile and mouthed, *Breathe*, which was a good reminder.

She reached out to shake hands with her dad. Was
that what one did at a moment like this, when parent
and child were total strangers? She didn't know. Her
head was still screaming.

Her mom came forward. She reached for Annie's
hands and squeezed them. "I can't imagine how over-
whelmed you must be. Come inside and have a sit-down.
I can make you a cup of tea or some cocoa."

Annie nodded, then wiped a tear away.

NASH HELD BACK as he watched the two enter the
house. Her dad stayed with him.

"Is she okay?" Mr. Ross asked.

Nash gave that question some thought. "That's easy
to ask but hard to answer. She's doing all right now.

She's healthy. Happy, I think. And loaded with baggage, as I imagine you both are."

Justin nodded. He tapped Nash on the back. "Well, let's go take the first step."

An hour later, Nash stood. "Right, so I think I'll head out." The four of them had been having a warm visit in the Ross' living room.

Annie frowned. "Nash. No. Don't go."

"I'm not leaving town. I'll be at a hotel near here. I'll text you the info." He shook hands with her parents. "It's been nice meeting you."

Mrs. Ross held on to his hand. "Nash, you're welcome to stay."

"Thank you. That's kind of you. But I think you need this time with Annie alone. A few days aren't going to make up for almost two lost decades, but they'll you set a foundation you can build on. You've got my number. Call if you or Annie need anything."

"I'll walk you out." Annie wrapped her arms around one of his as they walked down the driveway. "I don't want you to go."

"I'm not going to come between you and your family. You need this time with them. A few days, whatever. Give them that. We'll have the rest of our lives together. You and your parents have so much lost time to make up for."

"You'll call me?"

"No. You call me. I don't want to interrupt things. When you get a few minutes, call. Call before you go to sleep. Call when you wake up. Call me anytime." He smiled at her.

"A few days. That's it. I'm not moving in with them."

He smiled. That was good news. But who knew— maybe their visit would make that an appealing option. "Look on the bright side. Now you can wear pajamas."

She made a strangled sound somewhere between a giggle and a sob. "I was getting used to sleeping naked with you."

Fuck. "Me too. I put one of my T-shirts in your bag. Sorry—you'll have to wash it, but you can wear that until you go shopping."

She shook her head. "I'm not going to wash it. Ever. I want to have the smell of you if I can't have you with me."

"You'll always have me." He pulled her close. "I love you, Annie."

She reached up to hold his face. "Always?"

"Forever and ever. I'll text you where I'm staying."

"I love you, Nash. I can only do this because I know you're nearby."

"No. You can do this because you've dreamed of this your entire life. And you're one of the lucky ones who gets this chance. Enjoy it. Don't rush through it. I'm not going anywhere."

"What will you do while I'm here?"

Nash shrugged. "I don't know. Look around." He smiled. "Buy you pajamas."

"Are we going back to Harmony Falls?"

"That's a conversation we need to have. Maybe you want to be here?"

"I liked it there. It feels like we could be part of the start of something."

"I agree." He kissed her. "Now go be with your parents. And call me later."

NASH DROVE BACK through Old Town. When he stopped at a light, a store snagged his eye. A jewelry store. He pulled over and parked. This was seriously the craziest thing he'd ever done.

It also felt like the very best next step in his life.

He pulled out the bank card Charley left with him. Maybe there was enough to buy Annie's ring. If not, he had a nice nest egg and plenty of credit. But a little extra would be nice.

Using the login info she'd texted, he pulled up his account and stared in disbelief at the number he saw.

He texted Charley. *Is this a mistake?*

I told you what this job was worth to us.

Yeah, but he hadn't believed it. Who had that kind of cash lying around?

Shit.

We've already withheld your taxes from this payment. We're holding on to your paperwork in case you do another job for us this year.

Took Nash another moment to get his head around

the change in his circumstances. He and Annie really did have a wide-open future.

The store was brightly lit with shiny marble floors and wall-to-wall glass showcases. He walked around, trying to see some engagement rings without a herd of salespeople pouncing on him.

He found the display case with the rings, but just stood there. He could buy Annie a fucking boulder, but knowing her, she'd prefer a simple ring.

"May I help you?"

Nash looked at the woman on the opposite side of the counter. "I'm looking for an engagement ring."

The woman smiled. "That's exciting. For a woman or a man?"

That question surprised him, but he liked that she asked it. "Woman."

"Any ideas what she'd like? Simple? Ornate? What color gold? Platinum?"

He'd only seen Annie wear silver jewelry. "Simple. White gold."

"What's her ring size?"

"I don't know."

"Would you like to bring her in to help pick one?"

"No. I want to surprise her." He frowned. "Can I exchange it or return it if she doesn't like it?"

"We'll be happy to help."

"Okay. Then I want that one." He pointed to a simple solitaire with a round diamond.

She brought it out of the case and handed it to him. She started to explain that it was a two-carat diamond set in eighteen-karat white gold and what the diamond's cut, color, clarity values were, but he didn't care.

"I'll take it."

The woman looked shocked, then smiled. "I'll box it up for you."

ANNIE KNOCKED on Nash's hotel room door. It was late. She felt bad waking him, but she'd felt worse trying to sleep away from him. "Nash—it's me."

He opened his door. He looked pleased, then worried as he held the door open for her. "What's wrong?"

"Nothing." She dropped her things on a chair, then started to undress.

"I thought you'd be staying at your parents'."

"So did I. But I kind of panicked. I mean, not a bad bout of it, but I was frozen in place, staring at the bed. It was a shrine to my five-year-old self. I couldn't sleep there. My mom offered me another room, but I realized that I belonged here, with you." She slipped her jeans down and pulled her sweater off. "You're my home, Nash."

"Your folks okay with that?"

"I'm not a child. I've been on my own too long to go back now. But I told them we'd be over for breakfast."

"We?"

"We."

"Right." He kissed her. She pulled his tee off and

started on his baggy pajama bottoms. Just being near him, skin to skin, filled all the empty spots in her with love.

She couldn't get enough of him. Her hands were everywhere. She kissed his chest, his neck, his mouth. He walked them backward to the bed and dropped to the mattress, bringing her with him. She straddled his hips. Leaning over, she kissed him. He shifted then entered her. A shiver slipped over her. She stared into his eyes. He sat up and caught her face between his hands so he could kiss her as she moved over him. After a moment, she couldn't think, couldn't put words together in a rational way. She could only moan. He held her hips and lifted her just slightly, taking over the speed of their joining.

They came together.

Little ripples rolled through Annie for a bit. She was glad he was in no hurry to separate from her. She became aware of him watching her. She looked into his eyes and moved her thumb over his jaw.

"How was today?" he asked.

"Better than I could have ever imagined. I wasn't the only one who lost everything the day I was kidnapped."

"No, you weren't. Did you meet your sister?"

"She's coming over tomorrow."

Annie moved to her side and snuggled as close to Nash as she could, her face on his chest, his arm around her, his fingers lazily tracing patterns on her hip.

"Do you like your parents?" he asked.

"I do. They feel like I feel to me." She leaned up to

look at him. "I don't know how to explain it, but I feel like I belong with them."

He smiled. "That's the piece you've been missing."

"It is. I'm excited to meet my sister."

"Nice."

"Does this overwhelm you?"

"Nope. You?"

"A little. I'm used to being on my own."

"That's the thing about a family. It's best when everyone participates, just like a choir doesn't work with only one singer. It may be time for you to quit having one foot on the road, know what I mean?"

"I never wanted to be a runner. I always wanted to put down roots. It just wasn't a safe thing to do. Until you." She twined her fingers with his. "What about your family?"

"It's just me. My dad died in the first Iraq war. My mom passed while I was in the service. I'm glad we have your family."

THE ROSS HOUSE smelled delicious when they arrived the next morning. Annie's parents had been cooking up a feast.

"We didn't know what you two liked to eat," Vicki said.

Nash smiled. "Ma'am, I'm just out of the Navy. I eat anything."

"And everything you've made looks delicious to me," Annie said.

The front door opened and closed. A brown-haired version of Annie bounded up the steps. "I came as soon as I finished my test. I should have just blown it off and got out here yesterday." She stopped when Annie turned around. "Oh my God. They always said we looked alike." The two sisters hugged. They were both in tears when they parted.

"You're taller than me," Annie said. "And you have brown hair. Mine's dark red, when it's natural."

"And who's this tall drink of water?" Bree asked.

"Nash Thompson." He shook hands with Annie's sister. Her eyes were a little darker than Annie's, but her gaze was as penetrating. There was a lot of curiosity and a little wariness in her expression.

"You're the one who found her?"

He shook his head. "I wasn't looking for her. I was looking for the criminals who were looking for her. Long story."

"But he found us, and now we have Annie back," Vicki said.

Bree took hold of Annie's face. "I'm so sorry. It's because of me that you were taken."

Annie frowned.

"No," Justin said. "That was never true, Bree."

Bree started to weep. Annie put her arms around her. "We were at the community pool. It wasn't very big then. They've added a lot to it since that day."

"Bree was having a birthday party for her friends,"

Vicki said. "There were five of them in the pool. I didn't want to take my eyes off them, but you needed to use the restroom."

"I went with you, but I was annoyed I had to babysit you during my party. I left you in the bathroom." Bree sucked in a ragged breath and cried like her soul was shattered.

"I should have been there that day. But I went to work instead," Justin said.

"It wasn't your fault, not any of you," Nash said. "That belongs squarely on the heads of those who stole a child from a public restroom."

"What happened to them?" Justin asked.

"The law has them," Nash said.

"Too bad. I'd hoped they had died horrible deaths," Vicki said.

"I doubt they enjoyed the day they were arrested," Nash replied.

Annie's parents exchanged glances, then her dad nodded. "Good."

"Now who wants coffee?" Vicki asked.

AFTER BREAKFAST, Bree took Annie's hand and led her upstairs to her old room. Her sister looked around and frowned. "Aren't you staying here?"

"No. I'm staying with Nash at a hotel." Annie tossed one of the ruffles adorning the princess canopy bed. "I'm sorry you had to grow up with this."

Bree shrugged. "They kept it as it was when you left —not to blame me, but to remember you."

"But still…"

"I kept the door closed. I feel like I grew up that day, Annie. I've hated my birthday ever since."

Annie blinked away her tears. She'd cried so often this whole day—*everything* set her off again. "We all have so much healing to do."

"Yeah. We do. And so much to catch up on. Will you be staying in the area for a while?"

"I don't know. I think we'll be going back to Harmony Falls. I have a waitressing job there. But Nash and I haven't decided what's next. He's leaving that up to me. He's just out of the Navy and is having to start over too." She leaned closer to her sister. "He was a SEAL."

"A total badass, huh? I'm so glad you're with him. He seems really nice."

"He is. And Harmony Falls is just a few hours from here. So it will be easy to get together anytime. I can't believe all this time, when I've been here in Colorado, you guys were so close."

"I know. And all that time we've missed."

"But that's over now. I want to hear all about your life."

NASH COULDN'T BELIEVE he was so nervous to have a private conversation with Annie's dad. He was a friendly guy, but the stress of a life lived with a missing child had carved lines on his face prematurely.

Nash was worried about how he'd react to what he was about to ask.

"Mr. Ross, could we go outside for a minute?"

"Just call me Justin. You don't need to be formal with us."

Justin got a refill on his coffee, then they went outside to the deck on the back of the house.

Nash stood straight, his hands clasped behind his back, his legs slightly spread. "Sir, Justin, I know Annie and I haven't been together long, but in that time, we've already been to hell and back. I think we have a good sense of each other." Nash drew a deep breath. "I'm in love with your daughter. I'd like to marry her."

Justin's face didn't change expressions. He lifted his coffee and took a sip. "We've only just gotten her back. I don't want you to take her away."

"I will never take her from you."

"Where do you plan to live? You said you're just out of the Navy?"

"We haven't made our plans yet."

"You could stay around here."

"I think we're leaning toward returning to Harmony Falls."

Justin tilted his head. "That's only a few hours from here. We'd like having her so close. And you."

Nash stayed silent while Justin mulled the issue.

"Have you asked her yet?"

"No. But I bought the ring."

Justin smiled. "I have just one request. Can you ask her while we're with her so we can see her reaction? We've missed so much. I mean, we don't have to be in the room, but maybe we could be the first people she comes to when she shares the news?"

"Of course. She'd like that too. I don't know when I'm going to ask her, but I promise we'll be with you when I do."

"Good. Her mother will be over the moon. Having Annie back with us, getting to have her wedding... It's better than winning the lottery." He slapped Nash on the back. "Yes, son, I give you my permission. And I thank you for asking."

And right in front of Nash's eyes, the older man seemed to crumple. His shoulders hunched, he covered his face with his hand, and he wept.

"Oh. Hey. I didn't mean to upset you. I shouldn't have brought it up." Nash put an arm around Justin, feeling a little awkward.

Justin took a hankie out of his pocket to wipe his eyes and blow his nose. "That's not it at all. It's this day. I pretended to myself, and for my family, that it would happen one day. That our Annie would come home." He looked at Nash. "But to be honest, I'd given up hope." He shook his head and wiped his eyes again. "And now, we have everything. Our daughter back, the chance to get to know her, get to know you, get to have her wedding." He wept again for a moment, then cleared his voice and straightened. "Thank you."

"Don't thank me. I was just in the right place at the

right time and lucked into finding my heart there too. That any of this happened is because of how strong your daughter is. She survived. And now, I hope, she can thrive."

"I hope so too."

20

The February day was overcast, but the snow had stopped. Nash had been wanting to see the park by the falls on a day like this. He was glad that Annie hadn't needed much convincing. The dirt parking area had been plowed, and the path up to the falls had also been cleared.

Everything was going according to the plan.

Annie slipped her arm through his. She didn't look happy. "Anything wrong?" he asked.

She shrugged, then shook her head. "I'm just being stupid. I'd hoped to see it undisturbed, like we were the first people ever to find the falls. But someone else beat us to it."

He looked around. "Yeah, but we have a day together. That'll be fun."

She smiled. "True."

It wasn't only the parking area and the path in that were cleared; the picnic table and the area around it had been swept free of snow too. Sitting in the middle of the table was a glass vase filled with an arrangement of pink roses.

"Nash." Annie stopped abruptly. "I don't think we should be here."

"Why not?"

She nodded at the flowers. "Someone's having a private party."

"Oh. You think?"

She nodded.

"Ours was the only car parked back there," he replied. "Why don't we just go up to the falls and be there for a bit? If someone else comes, we can leave."

They walked up the path to where it widened by the falls. Everything there was dressed in snow—the boulders, the bare tree branches, the evergreen boughs. Sound was muffled. The half-frozen waterfall was less of a roar and more of a simple spill of water.

She closed her eyes and slipped her arm around Nash, leaning against him as she relaxed.

He'd been right. This was a magical place in the snow.

When she looked up at him, he tried to read what he saw in her eyes. She was his world, his everything. There was no fear in her expression—she'd grown in the time since they met. She'd dyed her hair back to its natural auburn color. Locks of dark red slipped over her white puffer jacket when she moved. She smiled more easily, laughed often, and stopped having panic attacks.

"Annie." He drew a breath. His face tightened. His

nerves were making her nervous. "There's something I need to ask you."

She pulled away from him and frowned. "Okay."

He gripped her hands and took a knee. She gasped, then started to laugh. He smiled at the beautiful sound of her joy.

"Will you marry me, Annie Ross?"

"Yes! Yes! Oh my God. Yes."

He stood, and she wrapped her arms around his neck. He laughed and swung her around then kissed her. He reached into his pocket and brought out a small velvet box. She bit her lip, waiting for him to open it. The ring was beautiful. A white gold setting for a simple solitaire, perfect for her, he thought. He hoped she'd love it.

When he slipped it on her finger, she squealed in joy. He laughed. She hugged him, then grabbed his arms. "We have to leave. We have to go right now and show everyone." She pulled him toward the path away from the falls. "Do you think my parents are home?"

"I don't know."

They went hand in hand back to the picnic table, but this time it was set with a tablecloth. Glasses of champagne were glistening next to the big bouquet. She looked at him, confused, but he just chuckled. Her parents, sister, Betty and Bernie, Caleb and Ruby, and Abel all slipped out from behind the big spruce where they were hiding.

Annie started to cry and laugh at the same time. Her mom hugged her, then everyone swarmed her.

"How did you put this together?" she asked Nash. "I was with you the whole time."

"It's been in the works a while. We were waiting for a weather report like this on a day everyone had off. Abel, Caleb, and Ruby cleared the snow and brought the flowers up ahead of time. Then they got your family and everyone hidden while I proposed." He smiled and kissed her forehead. "I love you, my sweet Annie." He looked into her eyes. "I want all our days to be this magical."

She nodded. "With you, they will be."

OTHER BOOKS BY ELAINE LEVINE

SHADOW SEALS

ROMANTIC SUSPENSE/MILITARY SUSPENSE

(This series may be read in any order.)

NOT MY SHADOW

SHADOW AND STEELE

O-MEN: LIEGE'S LEGION

PARANORMAL SUSPENSE

(This series must be read in order.)

LIEGE

BASTION

MERC

RED TEAM SERIES

ROMANTIC SUSPENSE/MILITARY SUSPENSE

(This series must be read in order.)

1 THE EDGE OF COURAGE

2 SHATTERED VALOR

3 HONOR UNRAVELED

4 KIT & IVY: A RED TEAM WEDDING NOVELLA

5 TWISTED MERCY

Sleeper SEALs

Romantic Suspense/Military Suspense

(This series may be read in any order.)

Men of Defiance Series

Historical Western Romance

(This series may be read in any order.)

ABOUT THE AUTHOR

Elaine Levine has a simple life and a twisted mind, both of which need constant care and feeding. She writes in several different subgenres of romance, including romantic suspense/military, historical western, and paranormal suspense. Her books are sexy, edgy, and suspenseful, but always end on a happy note because she believes love gives everything meaning.

Be sure to sign up for her new release announcements at http://geni.us/GAlUjx.

If you enjoyed this book, please consider leaving a review at your favorite online retailer and Goodreads to help other readers find it.

Get social! Connect with Elaine online:
Reader Group: http://geni.us/2w5d
Website: https://www.ElaineLevine.com
email: elevine@elainelevine.com